T0366041

SPIDERSILK
EXTENDED EDITION

AKUTRA-RAMSES ATENOSIS CEA

First edition 03/27/2013, Second edition 08/21/2013, Third Edition 11/26/2015

Order this book online at www.trafford.com
or email orders@trafford.com

Most Trafford titles are also available at major online book retailers.

Print information available on the last page.

ISBN: 978-1-4907-6810-6 (sc)
978-1-4907-6809-0 (e)

Library of Congress Control Number: 2015920446

Trafford rev. 12/19/2015

www.trafford.com

North America & international
toll-free: 1 888 232 4444 (USA & Canada)
fax: 812 355 4082

Contents

Introduction

WELCOME TO OLYMPUS. Mark Khiop has on3ly just moved in and plans on connecting with friends, starting with a house party. Mark is a contractor who develops video game worlds. The worlds are like other dimensions to Mark—dimensions where the player can explore another "thread" of the multiverse that we all live in. It is a place where there are other creatures to meet, as well as other players, and three dimensions are only the beginning. Not everyone is friendly, however, as Mark is soon to find out. Mark also delves into a very active dreamscape that he can interact with, much like the video games he designs. Mark not only likes designing his own universe "thread," he also loves exploring connections with others. The only questions are what cannot be designed and what connection cannot be bridged.

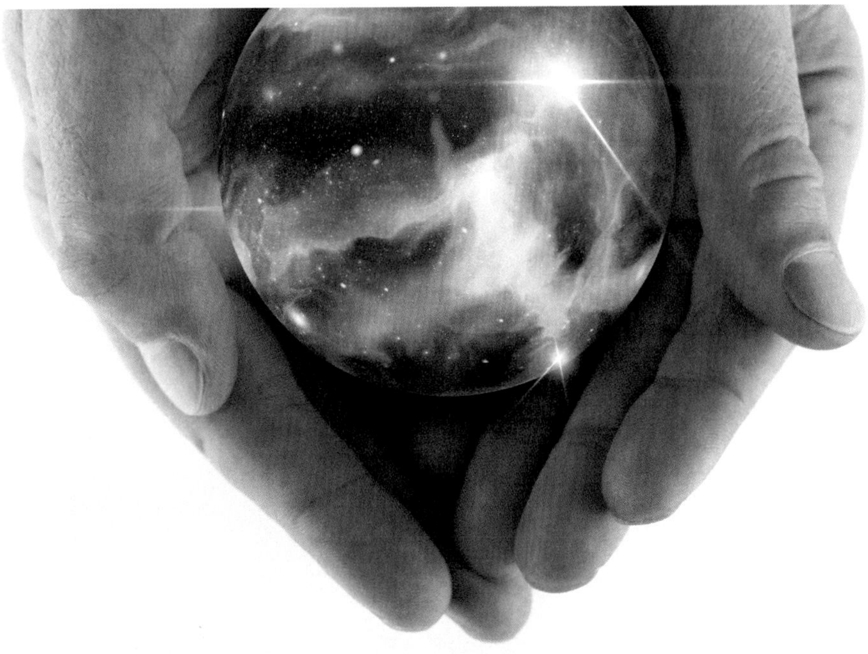

Chapter 1

Moving In

The dark browns mixed with black, and slivers of red seemed to dance ferociously to an endless depth within, as if his eyes were as vast as a galaxy. Mark's smooth skin provided a nice resting place for his trimmed shimmering auburn hair, having a shine that was nearly identical in color to his eyes. His slightly elongated face had some unique features, which Tia was scrutinizing. His full lips looked as if they were made for kissing. Tia turned and looked at the ceiling as she lay in the modern larger-than-king-size yet soft and silky bed. This was nice and it took quantum entanglement to a whole new level.

The patterns on the clean white ceiling where mere garnish for the thoughts she had meandering through her head. She tried to imagine what it would be like without Mark. He helped her in a plethora of ways to which he probably is not even yet aware. She grasped her sheets at the thought; her body snuggled with the comfort of the bed and sheets between. Turning again to gaze in Mark's direction she found no reason she should allow herself to break from this accord.

Mark had been equally scrutinizing Tia's long shiny black locks of hair and her soft lips. He had difficulty locating a blemish on her similarly smooth skin while admiring her puppy-dog green eyes. Marks heightened senses were tingling with high detail, and his inner-satisfaction was replete. The silk bed was so soft and comfortable, he thought to himself as he reached his hand under the sheets toward Tia's back where he lightly moved his hand, barely touching her skin. Responding with enthusiasm, Tia's lips reached for his, and they began the exploration of each other's faces.

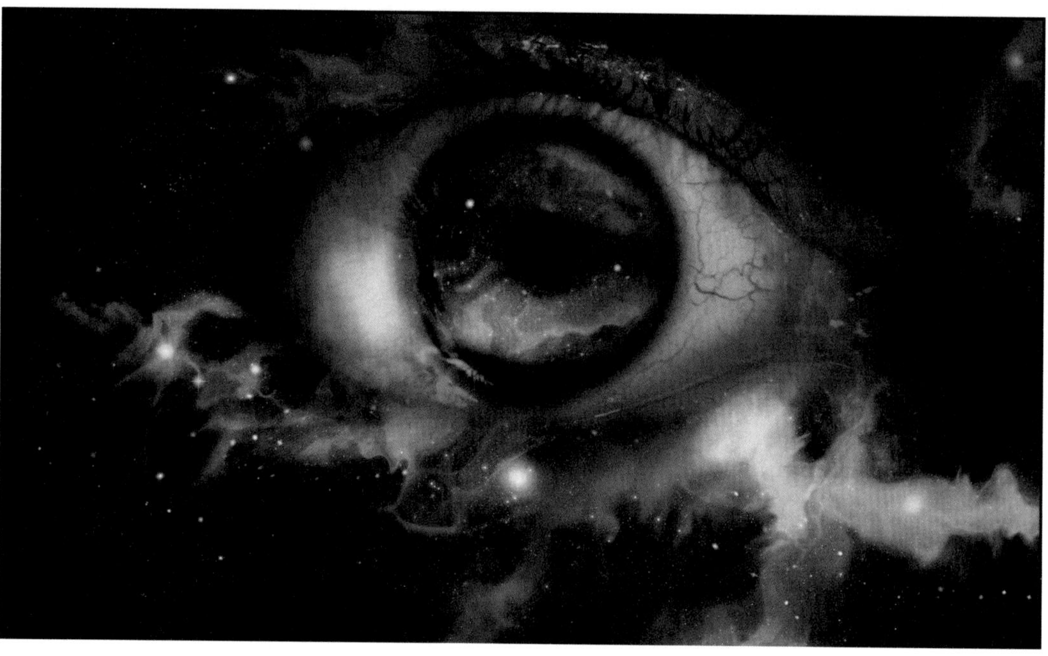

A loud sound interrupted the scene, and Mark opened his eyes with force. There he stared at the usual ceiling while reaching for his tablet with the intention of ending the loud alarm. "Those dreams are awesome," he muttered to himself referring to the vivid lucid dreams he regularly has. He had another code coordinate now—representation would match with what? Freeing himself from his silk sheets, he is up and extending to the bags of clothing not too far from his bed. Reaching back, he effortlessly tossed his throw blanket in a single toss on his bed, causing his bed to look like it was already made with neatly curved folds.

The bare white walls complemented the fresh carpet smell of the room he had slept in. Mark had barely begun to move into his newly acquired house, having signed the loan merely a few days ago. The clean sparsely furnished house gave the exciting vibe of future thrills and every detail could nearly tell its own story much like his current life. This house is full of possibilities he knew would be awesome. Mark whisked down the stairs while the soft velvety black carpet shimmered, satisfying his feet; he made his way to the brand-new kitchen.

Casually, with a sort of partial attention, Mark carved one scoop of espresso from the bag and started his morning cup. Navigating the maze of still-packed housing items, Mark reached for the mouse on his home entertainment system. Immediately, the TV began displaying the current video news from various Internet news sources. The system was preprogrammed to show news on certain topics and about specific things should they be found in the news sources.

Marks mini-tablet suddenly notified him of an incoming call. Answering the call Mark immediately views what appears to be a view from the sky, the large lake below was approaching at a high velocity. The air blew rapidly and suddenly a scream of joy. “Mark! What sizzles chizzle?” The high pitched under-duress voice revealed that she was either flying or falling. “Tina? To what end is the sky falling?” Mark finally queries. “Who else would send you a video while bungee jumping? I had to show you a glimpse of the rapidly approaching abyss. Mairis and I needed to rub it in a bit. See ya!” She disconnected, leaving Mark chuckling to himself. I’ll place that on my blog, he thought to himself.

The news showed pictures of the messed-up room of a house. “Intruders ransacked the house of Dacian Wilson. Dacian, a blind local resident, records the audio of his house, and the trespassers were apparently silent, leaving almost no trace on the audio recordings. It took police several hours to even detect the activity of the drawers opening when they stole personal articles. Puzzling investigators, the apparent thieves stole only a very few personal items, yet leaving the house ransacked." The newscast continued, eventually moving to the next story that muffled as Mark made his way toward the shower.

After a quick wash, Mark meticulously detailed his face, hair, and teeth before quickly tossing a neatly pressed shirt around his torso. He reached down and swiftly pressed his feet into a pair of thin leather slip-on shoes that snugly seemed to attach to his feet all the way to his ankles. Grabbing his car keys, he made an exit for his old yet gleaming green Acura TLX.

Shifting into gear, Mark was really comfortable in this car. He streamed down the small highway with extremely swift maneuvering actions, causing slightly thrusting movements. Slowing not nearly enough, Mark made a turn into the parking lot then came to a swift halt in one of the spots designated for his company.

Earlier that morning, Ramses had an unusually early visitor. Opening the enormous doors revealed an all-black figure which caused his white eye's to look that much brighter. Luminating the walkway before dawn several soft yellow lights allowed one to observe the fountain in the distance. Ramses' smiled at the sight of his visitor. "Did you find any artifacts of deliberate activities and associations?" The black stealthily clothed person adjusted his spandex facemask before responding. "Not much, merely the subtleties of the ghost within. That being said it may be what you need to send a sociable reply."

He reached into a black back-satchel and revealed a manila envelope then continued, "The optical discs have all the video we made, and the written report has everything else; all copies are on disc." Ramses placed a roll of credits in the masked figure's hand in exchange for the envelope then finalized the conversation. "You know nothing about these supposed events on this night nor Dacian." Closing the door, Ramses briskly made for his laptop. Now to assemble a full profile, he thought to himself.

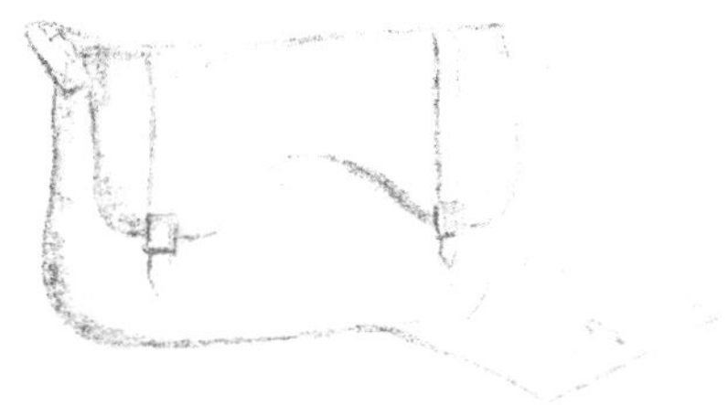

Swiftly browsing the disc Ramses gave a sigh then reached for his mango splashed with a bit of vodka. "The disc elaborated on it and he was correct, there really wasn't much found." Slowly sipping his drink, Ramses firmly grasped his forehead then gave a slight tremble. He thought to himself, it was imperative that he locate some particular that might lead to the discovery of what has happened upon Selene. Perhaps there was a lead or connection on the disc somewhere he could look further. Was she dead? It was difficult to fathom her simply leaving without notice.

Mark managed his mouse with ease, maneuvering the on-screen 3-D wireframe to various angles. The design aspect of this job was nearly completed, and he would soon need to find another contract. For now, he continued his task at hand. To his right, a slender lanky male in basic jeans and T-shirt sat, shifted back and forth while utilizing the mouse and jotting something on a tablet. His long dark-brown hair was flowing around as he repeatedly relocated it in order to continue what he was doing.

"How is the 'object positioning' progress?" Mark finally said with a smirk. "Fine, tedious work, but someone's got to do it," Tink responded in a sort of negative quiet tone. Everything had to align just right; otherwise, it would look odd during rendering.

Mark looked toward Tink, his eyes following Tink's movements. Smirking, Mark interrupted Tink. "Did you check the gamescape I made? What do you think?" Tink, pausing momentarily, said, "Yeah, besides working in it now, I took some time to 'check-it.' It is quite plush and detailed and should be a blast for the player." Mark stood and casually strolled to Tink's desk. He braced himself on Tink's desk, allowing him to easily share viewing of the screen. "You like the city? I call it Olympia. It rains a bit more frequently there, giving added game effects," Mark proudly commented then turned to gauge Tink's response. Tink smiled and responded, "Ah, Olympia? Not Olympus? It is good to show creative flare and I like the customizable treasure. As I said, it should be a blast." Mark smiled at the small comment on the name of the place while looking Tink directly in the eye. "Well nearly all natural things in this universe are made of repeating patterns. They repeat yet are slightly different. Think about it, its nature."

"Tink, will you 'show' at my housewarming party? I'm calling it the Face Reality Party so no drunken in-denial types can make it through the night," Mark elaborated while laughing. "Also, there is a dress code." Tink, showing genuine interest, swiftly turned to look him in the eye. "Dress code? No jeans, then? How much of it will be interpretable?" Tink's dark eyes and long hair make him look like he could possibly be Indian. "You can either be in costume or nice attire. No jeans, and there will not be any beer. Yea, people have various ideas on what 'code' is, it's for the picture you know what I mean. I want to learn as well as write a bit." Mark zapped. "I'll be there like an apparition," Tink responded assuredly, with absoluteness. Mark found that people seemed to show interest simply after he stated the dress code.

After a full day of work and organizing the house, Mark finally located his bed and shifted into a sleep state of mind. Mark found himself traveling along a mainland beach populated with palm trees. Looking inland, he pushed upward, immediately leaping high into the air. He began to soar a great distance, and he had complete control over direction. As he began to descend, he pushed upward again and leaped even without land underfoot. After traveling for some time, he came upon a small town. Here he descended in a controlled manner and landing with a hard thump, causing the ground to shake a bit.

Mark stood up and began walking through the dimly lit town, which was possibly somewhere in Colorado. A few streets down, there seemed to be some bad vibes echoing through the area. As if there was some sort of danger lurking. Mark decided to investigate and came upon some dark person or creature he could not discern its exact form.

Mark opened his hand, and in his palm, a large luminous question mark appeared. It turned with beady little yellow eyes, looking his way and slowly circling him. Suddenly, it dashed his way. Right behind it, another person knelt down, and a wave of gravel sprayed toward the feet of the approaching creature.

In the distance, there were two men in long flowing robes. They stepped on the corners of what appeared to be a large bright-blue padded mat. Standing, each of them lifted the shoulders of their robes, causing the robes to drop to the mat quickly. With swift moving limbs, they stood in a sort of kung fu defensive stance, obviously preparing to fight each other.

Mark swiftly focused his eyes, which became so hot that they emitted a thick luminous forceful wave. The creature, suddenly exposed by the light, was caught off guard. It hesitated out of shock and stumbled from the wave, grasping at where it was hit. At that moment, the wave of gravel pelted his feet, causing him to lose balance and fall backward to his backside. Very quickly, it jolted up and made for the hills in the distance. A crow, which had been sitting on a nearby tree branch, immediately made flight in the same direction.

Mark looked at the other boy and smirked as they high-fived. Fireworks illuminated the background as they conducted a victory handshake. Garrick was someone Mark seemed to frequently meet while dreaming these very real lucid dreams. He had come to recognize him as a worthy ally and collaborator. Suddenly Mark opened his eyes to his plain white-walled room.

Chapter 2

Tragic Leap

One year earlier…

Chris held the recorder near his mouth and said, "Today was a good day. Financial numbers are up, quality numbers are up and cost are down. The new 'Explorer IV' power tool is selling nicely, now to ensure that the 'Explorer V' can top it. I must discuss it with our technology investors." Releasing the record button he pondered his approaching plans. Damn—Those technology investors. I would be very rich right now if they did not have me one over. Thoughts, lingered in his mind.

Chris's office was a modest 100 square feet with a this wooden desk against the back wall. The computer interface was the basic brail keyboard with pointer and sound graph renderer ear piece. Chris, however, really liked his thin mesh flexible rolling chair.

Suddenly his senses tingled, and he noticed an approaching person. It was Dacian, Chris could tell by the texture he was sensing. Dacian's heavy thrusting firm actions and slightly brutish meander could be recognized easily. Especially to Chris who has known him for a time. Chris reached for his 'range scanner' and placed it in his ear. Dacian had just opened the slightly oversized wooden door. "Hello, Chris! How is it?" The slightly thick person standing just inside the doorway was a friend and technical advisor of Chris's.

Chris faced Dacian and responded, "Well, you know. Numbers are up and costs are down, so pretty well." The odor of Dacian was fresh and he had obviously recently showered. "Are your technology guy's still 'raykin' most of the credits?" Dacian laughed, he had discussed this with Chris on numerous occasions. Chris merely chuckled and mumbled as his response which implied a 'yes'.

Dacian sighed with a positive tone. “Listen, I need to discuss something with you that came up on one of our exploration radar sensors. No hurry, can we schedule something for tomorrow? Say, 10?” Chris smiled to himself which Dacian could probably detect. “Yes, that sounds great! It’s been a while anyway and we could catch-up. Meet me here, and we’ll breeze to the Waverider for brunch and coffee or something.” Dacian turned toward the exit. “I’ll be there. Talk at you later!”

Feeling around Chris located his secure access device, jacket and walking stick. Swiftly rising, Chris made for the exterior where his ‘traveler’ was stationed. Chris recalled his grandfather rambling on about how the first travelers were. While amazing transporters, they initially could only be utilized by the few ‘seeing’ people since they were so dangerous. Numerous bugs in the navigation and range sonars required backup scanners or someone who could understand what was happening. He laughed at that, how primitive life must have been.

Approaching his front door, Chris’s range scanner advised him that it had unlocked and was opening as the sensor was programmed to do upon detecting Chris. A nice fresh scent was in the air, yet Chris could detect some pattern forming that may be less pleasant. Briskly stepping inside, Chris could sense the smell and form of his slender companion, Ekaa. “Heelloo! How was your day?” Chris cheerfully sounded. Turning toward Chris, Ekaa responded with an unsteady tone. “Just incredulous now that you are here!”

Chris responded in kind. “That is stupendous. Is there anything else you need to say? Is there something wrong?” Ekaa softly grabs Chris’s hand then sits down on the couch with him. “It’s Darven. He is so smart, and has been achieving good enough grades to go to a really nice university. I was thinking of trying to get him into Boxington Wave. I know it is a bit far away, but it is for the best.” Chris contemplated that briefly then responded. “That is one of the more expensive schools and will be difficult to afford with everything else going on.” Ekaa whined and mumbled a bit. “I KNOW! It’s tha-that, I want to enable him to attain a good future. Better than we have if possible.

Chris reached for his mouth and softly rubbed it while considering his financials. “Darn, if those—damn—technology investors didn’t take so many credits. I mean—the company is doing well right now. It’ll take time to attain the extra funds.” Ekaa mumbled a bit again. “I don’t think Darven has time. Really standard grades complete in one year at the most two, and he will need to start within the first year after or he’ll get a slow start in life. You know how that goes, kids who get a slow start!?" Chris turned and fiddled with his lips. "Hmmm---yes, slow start is less time to enjoy and sometimes more difficult. I'll try to think of something."

Ekaa then responded with positivity. "Well let's eat dinner and sound graph a movie. I'm a bit tired and would like to relax into rest period." Chris smiled and breathed sharply. "That is a great idea for an ending to this day."

Dabbling in his coffee, Chris queried Dacian. "So, what is going on that we need to discuss?" Dacian sounded excited as he responded. "Well, we have some very odd readings from one of our deep woods sonar. It's reading all kinds things that should not be there. We even collaborated with a Romadium team to run scans from the other side of the forest, and guess what?" Chris still not sure responded. "More unusual readings?" Dacian still excited. "They did not detect us. In fact the sensors gave a readout that suggested there was a body of water in the location we should have been detected, or liquid of some sort. I think we need to send in a scouting team."

Chris quickly recognized where this was going. "Sounds great! When do we go check this out?" Dacian flags the waiter for more coffee then responds. "How about tomorrow?!" Now Chris is interested. "Ok, so let me get this correct. The sensors detect all sorts of things that are sort of normal yet should not be in that location, and they do not detect things that are there?" Dacian laughed at the bizarre nature of that. "Yes! It's like the detection waves are not getting through or something." Chris sips his coffee. "Or it is getting readings from far away and somehow confusing them. Interference?" Dacian intensifies, "I thought of that. What would be that powerful to interfere with all of our sensors? Even the Romadium sensors?"

Chris flags the waiter. "Charge please." Then he turns toward Dacian. "I'll locate a few people that should go with us on this trip. You make shuttle arrangements."

"Ever been outside of Braila?" Chris queried his friend John Cords while paying attention to every detail of his bio-patterns. "Me? No, not ev-aa. All my business has been here until this point. My parents used to travel to the Black Ocean for outings. After we acquired a nice pool, I have simply been too busy to frolic as such. I can frolic in town save on transport time." John said while chuckling a bit. Chris sympathized with extra use of time then responded. "Well, we are about to go to the edge of the state of Vular. Specifically it is somewhere near the Titu Forest and not far from the border with Romadium."

Dacian announced himself as he whisked by. "Time to board the shuttle! You'll like these private shuttles; it is one perk of a VIP agency account." Swiftly grabbing their gear, Chris and John followed. "About how long is the flight? Do you know?" John zapped. Slightly pausing, Dacian responded, "It's a two hour flight."

The craft had several large comfortable seats to choose from. "Nice seating, man!" John stammered. They shortly settled, and without delay were departing the private landing pad. "Here we go!" Chris toasted to a safe and successful trip.

Forty-five minutes into the trip, Chris could suddenly hear one of the engines sputtering. "What is that?" Chris swiftly stammered. Dacian turned towards him. "I am sure they are prepared for small contingencies,

I'll check with the pilot." Briefly returning, Dacian sounded assured. "Some debris was stuck in the engine. They restarted it to break it free. They advised me it was nothing they could not handle."

The shuttle resumed smooth flight until suddenly jolting and jerking with force. "What the heck is that?" John is the first to respond this time. Dacian was already on it and trying to brace himself as he stumbled toward the flight control area. After a few moments he returned. "A freak storm appeared out of nowhere. I mean it was not on radar and then it was suddenly right in front of us." Chris was about to say something when there was a large crackling electrical noise. Within moments everything went quiet except the outside storm.

"Did we lose power?" Chris screamed. "That we did. Brace for impact." Dacian responded swiftly. Emerging from flight control an assistant announced, "Please, everyone remain calm. Brace for impact according to the safety procedure protocol. Air breathing apparatuses are in the left arm of your seat and if you need it the seat cushion will act as a flotation device."

Chapter 3

The Party

After finalizing the placement of his furniture and equipment, Mark's house was finally furnished and ready for tonight. Mark set up the door equipment as the sushi and hors d'oeuvres arrived via his good friend Ramses. "You're up! Are you ready for the approaching boiler?" Ramses's slightly wavy jet-black hair wisped lightly on his head. His thin dark eyebrows complemented his deep-seated dark-brown eyes and his smooth permanently tanned skin. His hair was cut very short near the neckline and was progressively longer until the bangs, which flowed to his forehead. He sported a shiny blue-and-black rayon shirt with a solid brass zipper zipped down just enough to expose a smooth lightly muscular chest and some gold necklaces.

Mark, still in his silk robe, smiled. "Almost.. now that the hors d'oeuvres have arrived. This is going to be huge. I am preparing for a possible atomic reaction." Ramses chuckled and comically continued, "You can always knock their heads out if necessary; extra materials for the rest of us. Did you assemble the video for the wall screen?" Hanging all around Ramses was Tina. Rubbing his forearm she leaned on him. "We're going to make the Qi of this place pulsate!" Tina zapped while actively moving about and gripping Ramses.

Mark stepped outside to obtain an immediate sensory readout. It was a warm sunny day, birds flapping about could barely be heard in the distance. The air was unusually light and crisp yet felt fresh as the heat of the sun warmed his skin like the perfection of the day thus far. In the distance, a single lenticular cloud provided an odd sensation. Suddenly out of the corner of his eye he noticed a ferret. With a flash it swiftly chased what appeared to be a lizard of some sort possibly a sandstone night lizard. Mark remarked while alerting Ramses, "How unusually dapper is that?" Ferrets are animals Mark considered quite posh.

Ramses smirked in a playfully lofty manner, "An opulent omen! If I was superstitious, I would only hope that the animal's chase does not refer to some sort of issue ahead." Tina smiled fondling and squeezing Ramses, "A good omen indeed!"

Mark laughed at Tina's playfulness. He knew she was not dating Ramses, yet you could hardly tell if it weren't for the lack of kissing. Mark had a large video screen covering one of the walls, which he planned on playing a sequence of art, music videos, and movie clips. Mark smirked and jokingly responded, "Most certainly and those that drink too much might make it to the morning as extra breakfast for the nobles and peasants. Right now, I am setting up the badge printer. As they pay the cover charge entrance fee, we will print a custom badge with their signature and name surrounded by the party imagery and slogan." Ramses smoothly returned, "Ah yes, the Faces of Reality Party, and what exactly is reality?" Mark laughed again, "Our epic adventure of course as it does not require a delusion of the mind."

People were arriving at a rapid pace even with a ten-dollar entrance charge. Party masks were everywhere. The masks that Mark had made with the party imagery were selling out fast. Even the light rayon jackets with the party slogan were selling rapidly. Mark was exceedingly pleased that none tried to enter while not meeting the dress code, and all looked reasonably attired. Champagne and martini glasses frequented hands everywhere as the rooms slowly began to over-capacitate.

"That is an exceptional piece of depth," a slightly thick five-foot-nine white male said with a prideful gleam, his brow showing small amounts of moisture. His short blond hair was slightly messy yet matched well with a light-beige sports jacket and dress pants. Mark smirked, lifting his head loftily, purposely attempting to please and encourage while responding, "Hello, Josh, it is a little rough around the edges, yet most certainly exquisite. It looks even better with a little hard work. Careful on getting close to it; wild animals within may decide to explore your world." Josh chuckled. "Well, when I repay you in full, I want it back looking excellent as ever wild animals and all." Mark smirked, moving his right hand in a reassuring manner. "Absolutely, the only thing that would change that is failure to pay…" Laughing, he continued slightly sarcastically, "at that point it's mine to recycle if I so please."

"Did you set up that sequence?" A female stated in a raised voice. Mark turned attempting to locate the source. A lightly peppered smooth-skinned young woman stood in front of him pointing to the wall video. Her hair was a shiny shimmering black, complementing her dark-green eyes. She was conveniently holding in her hand a nearly empty martini glass with a solitary olive.

Mark looked her over and said, "Yes, I did. If pictures are like a thousand words, it is a vast novel. You like it? Can I get you another drink?" Isis's slightly raccoon-like eyes shifted to the side with a slightly smirking smile, even though she was clearly thinking about Mark. The large screen was playing a combination of atmospheric, tech, and dubstep music, mixed with famous art, famous places, music videos, and movie clips. "That's awesomely riveting, nice synchronicity. I'm Isis, by the way. Sure, I'll take another. Apple martini? Actually, this place is very quiet for the sheer quantity of people."

Mark pressed his headset and requested an apple martini then turned to Isis. "Isis, like the Egyptian goddess? Nice name. You like the masks I made for the party?" Isis turned and looked at him. "I'm wearing one of the masks, aren't I? Are we supposed to only show the side of us that fits the party theme?" Mark chuckled, "Other than behavior befitting the party, you can show whatever side you so desire." Isis turned to Mark. "This party is lavish do. You should render party entertainment in 3-D space more like a video game. That way, you can kill it with your computer skillz." Mark laughed, "I could have rendered guests as well as physical ones!" Then he continued inquisitively, "How did you know about my computer, uh . . . skillz?" Isis smirked loftily. "You said you did the sequence of the video, and it's succulently hot. The music selection synchronized smoothly with the video and also provides a bit of mystery, causing me to ponder researching the presented imagery. It is fascinating. I'll be back. I have to go attend to one of my friends." Mark smiled slightly comically. "Uh-oh. Nobody should drink too much. It isn't wise, and may require you to take over." Isis smiled as she slipped away.

Mark escaped to the bathroom for a moment. He touched up his hair in the mirror, and was generally very detailed. Mark lifted a Mark Izh-79 weapon from under his arm; checked and cleaned it slightly. The teargas bullets were still intact. Suddenly, Mark heard something odd coming from a dark corner of the large bathroom near the walk-in shower area. "Why so silent?" it said. Mark, a little startled, slowly moved toward the dark area; nothing physical was there. "Is someone there? Come out and show your face!" Mark said demandingly. The voice responded, "You're not real. What are you hiding? Why so quiet? What do you have to hide? We feel if we say too much we may be revealing to those that say little." Mark, now disturbed, walked over to where the voice was coming from. This was very startling because there was nobody, except him, in the entire bathroom. It was a "voice," wow! I have not heard a spiritual voice since old gramps went crazy listening to them, Mark thought. That was not good, yet Mark was skeptical of them. Ah well, who cares. It was probably attracted to the quantity of people, he thought as he exited.

Mark waltzed into the kitchen-and-den area, which was also loaded with people. It was very slow moving since he had to greet nearly every person as he moved through the party. Mark edged up to a finely detailed male whom he recognized as Rae Osira. "Rae, how are you this fine adventurous eve?" Rae turned towards him then brightened his expression while reaching for a handshake. "Your auspicious event flows like a roaring flame yet runs like a well-oiled machine!"

"With absolute certainty, well put Rae. The atmosphere seems as though a kinetic mystical event is taking place. Only time will tell the quantum results this event will have." Standing next to and almost, yet not quite, hanging on Kara was Tina with a beaming smile. Tina chuckled in a general seductiveness manner clearly meant as a visual appetizer yet not directed at anyone. Tina continued, "I wish office parties were this suave and artful. I must try to convince Siv to improve on his atmosphere. Perhaps, I should ask Mark to help." Mark smirked a bit then replied, "Yes, I do like a smooth atmosphere. Thank you very much."

"Kara, what do you think of the projected video sequence?" Turning her head, Kara's gleaming eyes were unmistakable under the party mask. "Nice tech, Mark. I really like the projected content; it really synchronizes with the flow. You seem rather astute in technology, something Rae is very fond of as well." Seductively gripping Marks bicep while simultaneously stroking her upper thigh Kara continued, "Rae could always use profitable friends in his investments, you should come over and visit sometime." A gleam in Rae's eye clearly shows approval of such behavior from Kara. Mark responded smoothly, "Most certainly my friend, I'll check my schedule and we can coordinate a collaborative socialization."

Interrupting Rae, Tina interjects, "Mark, please drop a visit to Mairis and I sometime." Looking at Rae and Kara, Tina bids them ado. With a light smile Rae continues, "Yes, yes. Did you finish the landscaping in that video game environment…uh, Olympia, right?" Mark zaps back, "Well, almost. Shortly it will be." Rae sips his martini then reaches into his pocket for his tablet. "Sort of like the environment in this house and the landscape of its yard. The Qi is smooth. Flow-masters like you always seem to design lush environmental scenes and landscapes." Reaching Kara, Rae steps a little closer and snaps a few pictures with his tablet.

Mark noticed Ramses a short distance away as he shook Rae's hand. Like rocket science, Mark made for an approach, Ramses looked his way. "Mark! Spectacular party, there seems to be much available space if I were to crawl along the ceiling! I think the door guy is turning people away due to capacity. This is absolutely astounding." Mark smirked at the compliments. "I have a nice profit margin, I am sure. All the masks and jackets have sold." Mark looked at the corner where the TV was playing financial news. "Who the heck is watching that? My party attendees aren't exactly bottom of the barrel." Ramses' face was gleaming the oil on his face mixing with the sweat of his brow. Ramses laughed with a smirk. "Yeah, I noticed that. You should be sure to get business cards, opportunities must be among them." Turning to look Ramses in the eyes, Mark confidently responded, "I made sure the door guy annexes them already."

Further meandering around, Mark noticed Mairis and Tina. "How are you this fine festive moment in time?" Tina jumps raising her hands in the air. "Mark! We are rocking out to your dubstep, we've already created a temporary dance area twice. How goes the flow?" Pausing for a moment Tina continues, "You have such beautiful eyes." Mark nodes while slightly rubbing his chin. "Considering that idea, why don't we dance?" Moments later, they were locked in rhythm as best as the girls could loosely maintain.

A few hours passed quickly as Mark tried to socialize with as many people as possible before finally returning to Ramses vicinity. Suddenly, Isis showed up squeezing through the crowd. "Hello, Mark. I told you I would return." Return she did; she had a girlfriend with her named Shara. Shara immediately attached herself to Ramses who was standing next to Mark. Isis, who was just shy of six feet, immediately smothered Mark. They were obviously slightly intoxicated yet not quite drunk, which Mark was glad of. "Can we escape to the upstairs room?" Isis seductively chimed. Mark turned to Ramses with a slightly aloof raised eye brow and a laugh. "See you on the morrow."

Isis casually rolled into her usual parking lot where she located her parking spot as if she was on autopilot. She quickly noticed her brother Geb's large SUV in one of the free spots. There is nothing quite like a nice morning of brotherly razzing, she thought mildly laughing to herself. The purr of her satisfying car came to a halt as she swiftly made for the townhouse.

Opening her unlocked door, Isis quickly located Geb sprawled out on the crème couch a large coffee in hand partially watching a sporting event. "Ah, I see sister discovered her way home again." Isis chuckled at the sarcasm while locating a comfortable place for her purse. "Geb, what is of the utmost on T.V. that brought you to this abode of mine?" Geb laughed and turned to look at her rather than the T.V. while lightly covering his mouth with his hand. "Truly, amusing. How was he?"

"Mark? He was most certainly enjoyable. An air of sophistication mixed with a sort of cyber spinner." Isis gleefully elaborated while accessing the refrigerator for an energy beverage. "Everything going as planned then, good. I merely wanted to ensure all was well after that." Geb responded while casually examining his lightly unshaven face for blemishes in the small reflective statue end piece. "Well, you know. I usually get what I want." Isis smirked loftily while changing the channel.

Isis continued, "I did seem to notice a sense of mysterious possibilities. In his house, in his eyes and pretty much everywhere. It's fine though, it's not like I know him well enough yet to pry. I got the distinct feeling there was a LOT more to him than I had immediate access to and every detail was a clue. Really, that only added to the excitement of the moment."

Geb reached for Isis' arm and clutched it with a tenacious grip. "I am serious. Some of those guys may be more dangerous, powerful and ferocious then you expect. They don't always play like nice little gentlemen." Isis swiftly turned looking into his earnest and concerned dark brown eyes. She noticed a slight tear mixing with the oils at the corner of his eye. "Bro" She said softly, barely above a whisper. Geb continued, "You know, I'll always be there for you like I am here now." Isis smiled with sincerity and continued in a low tone. "I know bro. I know. Mark was ...cultivated." Geb releasing her arm smiled. "I must be on my way. Sett is waiting for me."

Chapter 4

Contact

Mark, sitting in front of his computer, was browsing through the gameplay schematics. The game was an MMO (massively multiplayer online game) where each player would need to decipher symbols, communicate through symbols, best other players in combat, discover treasures, and even create treasures. Prized treasures would often increase in value over time. While players could communicate with one another in the usual way, there were parts in the game where players would have a distinct advantage while utilizing silent symbolic communication. He particularly enjoyed placing secret treasures and portals for the players to discover.

Taking a break, he opted to check his bank account for his most recent paycheck. He quickly checked his tablet sitting next to him. A high resolution seven-inch mini tablet with projector, it was beyond excellent for the task. To his surprise, his account had minimal funds. "What?" Mark mumbled to himself as he quickly browsed to several of his private project accounts. The large party profits he most recently deposited also seemed gone. A tingle on his neck turned into a slight jitter as Mark decided to look into the activity detail.

Scrolling through the transactions, Mark located three withdrawals of various amounts. The withdrawals nearly entirely depleted his account. Several thousands of dollars were gone. "Fortunately, most of my money is in an investment account unless they got that too," he muttered again to himself. The transactions were odd. The first transaction was from "You're not real." The second transaction was from "We will find everything out." The third transaction came from "There is nowhere to hide." Mark was like, 'what the?', and he immediately called the police as well as his banking institution.

"Check . . . this . . . out, Tink," Mark, slightly jittery, slowly stated with a deep tone while looking at his tablet. Tink, looking at the computer screen, was enthralled in something and slowly pulled himself away,

"Huh?" Mark, swiftly looking up, said, "You must check this out." Mark was now calling the police on the side bar of his tablet.

Tink swiftly rolled over to Mark in his chair. "What's up?" Mark motioned to his Smart Tab. Tink examined the content and then, with intensity scrutinized the screen suddenly responding, "Wow! What the? Someone is playing with your head. A hacker perhaps, but why?" Tink looked up. "Calling the police? What a trip. I hope you catch them." Tink then turned and returned to his computer.

Reaching for his keys, Mark breezed toward his parked Acura. The sun was setting on the horizon, and a brilliant display of colors flooded the sky. Mark was the last one to leave the office today and could not wait to get home. Suddenly, a loud hissing noise seemed to come from right behind him. Instantly, it seemed to stream to and fro all around him and his car, sort of like the wind or a gas. Even more surprising was when it seemed to talk. "Soon we will have it. You cannot hide." There was obviously nothing physical where the noises were coming from. "You have ways of saying things that truly make those such as myself understand you. Picking a fight with things you seem to have difficulty reading is not always the wisest of strategies. Why bother?" Mark jabbed as he started his car to make an exit.

Driving along at a few miles over the speed limit, Mark pondered the odd encounter his heart rate slightly elevated. It could have been worse. Suddenly, Mark noticed some strange pain in his head. Like a head ache he had never experienced before. A black mist descended over his eyes and Mark began to swerve, struggling to maintain control of the vehicle he released the accelerator. Barely missing an oncoming vehicle, Mark reflexively swerved to the side of the road slamming on the breaks.

The pain intensified and streamed down his face. Reaching for his head with his hands, Mark connected to deep inside his head and being. Sweat began beading from his forehead wetting his clothing and gushing in what seemed like a small stream. Out of what appeared to be necessity for the moment, Mark pushed from within with a ferocity he had not shown for some time.

Very shortly, his physical face changed slightly and his third eye exposed its self. The black mist rescinded nearly instantaneously. Utilizing his 'eye' he could see all sorts of dark mists around him. In the near distance was again a black scraggly straight haired hyena. The hyena was not growling, it stood under a drooping bush like tree with yellow flowers. Like a cloud, a large quantity of golden moths resided in the tree, and a few of them flew away.

"What is upon us? What are these black gas clouds or mists? At preset they appear formless." Mark pondered the sight he beheld and the hyena was another oddity. A single moth landed on the hood of his car. Mark scrutinized his surroundings, where were his spiders? He turned and surveyed the insides of his Acura. Sure enough, there they were several spiders he was used to seeing yet they were not outside for some reason. Regaining his composure, Mark accelerated rapidly toward home.

Entering his house, Mark took extra care to be as silent as possible. These things most likely utilized their ears since they seem to prefer dark places. Was it the ghosts of those so-called voices that plagued his grandfather? Grandfather was clinically diagnosed shortly after that. At least, I don't think I am going crazy, this is very real. Why did his grandfather so desire to communicate with them? Mark often wondered what grandpa would have been like without them which did not guarantee sanity.

I must keep those annoying things out. I rarely say that, yet these odd voices are not to his liking. They seem to have malicious intent and they intend on stealing, was all he could think. Still being off the radar as far as noise, Mark reached for a nightcap before ending the evening in bed. The liquid made some noise as he poured it over the ice in his cup, and Mark hoped it would not matter when suddenly, from a dark corner, a voice said, "Found you!"

Mark, with a jerk, spilled a small amount of whiskey. He turned toward where the voice came from. "Get out of my house," he said. The low raspy voice continued, "Very clever being silent. It won't work. Sooner or later, you will make noise." Mark, very irritated, said, "I'll tell you what won't work. The little trick you pulled with my bank account. My bank will refund me the monies, and the police will hunt down your little hacker friend." The voice continued calmly, "Oh, that? That's only a little sample. The police won't find him. We're going to take more of your stuff when you least suspect it."

It clearly did not feel as though "they" could take whenever "they" wanted to, and therefore, it was either studying him or not strong enough for a brute-force attack. Mark had enough of this 'dialog'. "Now get out of here before I send my minions over there to finish you. I'd do it myself if I wasn't busy getting this beverage." With that, there was not another sign of whatever or whoever it was.

Was this in his head? It sure did not seem that way; not at all. Mark carefully scanned the room and whistled a tune. Still no response from what seemed to be the little 'dark one' or anything else for that matter. Rinsing his glass he alertly made his way to his room while paying attention to every detail available to him.

With a small leap, Mark landed with relief in his silky smooth memory foam bed. The memory foam was soft yet firm all at the same time, making for a satisfying sensation, especially when Mark was mentally prepared for bed. Shifting states, his thoughts faded into the dream plane where Mark was waving to Tink while exiting to a small dusty path. Suddenly, he recognized something—or someone rather. It was Isis. She was somewhere around here, yet was not visibly present.

Mark continued down the dusty trail and then decided to take a momentary break to look around the immediate area. There was a solitary tree standing a short while away, alone yet it did not look unhealthy with vibrant green leaves. He thought to himself, why this road all the time? A dusty dirt road would it symbolize a place of low population, perhaps it is not maintained? He looked at the road and it appeared neat despite lacking blacktop. Clearly the edges appeared trimmed by someone not too long ago, perhaps a country road to private places.

Suddenly, there were giant PlayStation-sized spiders all around him. Several of them were spinning webs. Mark peered closely at one; he could sense the non-human thing that it was. Was it logical, smart, or primitive? They seemed actually very intelligent, with possibly a "munster" sort of intelligence, and it responded to him. Immediately, it sort of lay flat on the ground in a sort of non-threatening way. The others made a sort of circle around him, moving with his movements. Mark laughed; he loved his house and continued walking the trail.

In the distance, there was lightning and very quiet thunder, which seemed to almost strike some rickety wood and stone objects. The area where this was occurring seemed particularly less hospitable. A few crows rested on various objects that were tall yet-unrecognizable forms. Was this the place where the "voices" were? Had he found them?

Mark approached the location, and the previously silent crows announced his arrival. The "voices" did not say anything, yet that did not mean they weren't there. The crows could be their alarm system for all he knew. Something began to beat like an old Indian drum, yet there were no "words" of spoken language. He looked around and noticed that the nearby spiders made no response whatsoever to the "noise." A dream catcher blew in from the wind, landing perfectly on a solitary wooden post that seemed to signify a sort of official entrance to the seemingly barrier-less zone, a single drop of water attached to the weaves of thread at its center.

Without warning, standing next to him was Tia, smiling seductively. She always had a little lust in her eyes when she looked at him, and he had many dreams of her. For some reason, he seemed to think she lived in a different thread of the multiverse. In his version, she did not physically exist. Even though it may be slightly odd, he found no reason to dispute it unless she simply lived in the dreamscape. Tonight, she seemed particularly pleased with herself. She reached into her pocket and revealed a key, handing it to Mark. The key fit perfectly in a small spot on the dream catcher.

Suddenly, a warm sensation came over Mark's eyes, causing him to open them to the usual ceiling. Mark, with a jolt, was wide awake, yet somehow he desired to pursue that dream a bit further. What the heck was that place, and was it friend or foe beyond the post entrance? Such things were thoughts that he pondered through his mind as he prepared for work.

Mark's custom doorbell started announcing the arrival of a guest. "How can I help you?" Mark jabbed. Standing at the door was a clean-cut six-foot male with sturdy yet neat and warm thick clothing. Mark thought to himself, this guy's a skeptic, not really a bad thing. "I am Officer John Thomas, and I am here to take your statement concerning the fraudulent charges on your account." "Oh, great. Basically, charges suddenly appeared on my account. I am really not sure how they made those charges. Nothing was stolen or missing," Mark confidently explained in brief.

The officer looked seriously at Mark. "Have you had any suspicious contacts that may have had anything to do with this?" Mark looked slightly upward in contemplation. How was he to explain everything? That would be an odd story.

"You know, I did experience someone who said 'You aren't real.' It was said in a suspicious manner to me, similar to what the credit card charges stated." In a slightly skeptical yet serious scowl, the officer responded, "Really? Did you happen to notice anything unique about them? Possibly a description?" Mark was not quite sure about this; it was a voice, after all, and no visible description had been ascertained. Mark responded, "No. Actually, I did not see their face, only their voice—kind of deep and raspy. For the most part, I shrugged it off at the time." The officer, clearly not sure if Mark was divulging everything, said, "Only a voice, huh? Okay, well, that will go in my report. Do you have any opponents or foes that might consider doing this to you for any reason?" In contemplation, Mark responded, "Well, I do throw some reasonably sized house parties. Anyone at the party could think of me as a monetary target. Other than that, I don't know." The officer smiled. "We will consider all possibilities. Thank you for your time, and have a good day."

Chapter 5

Investigations

Walking briskly to his car, John peered to his right and smirked. Another detective Eurus responded with a lite smile. “Odd, wouldn’t you say that there was no description?” Slightly frowning John replied. “Not really.” Eurus sensing that there is more to this swiftly goes on, “It seems as though you should brief Kratos on this one.”

After returning to the brilliantly reflective large grid like building known as H.Q. John exited toward the main entrance. John was thinking, the smart parking spots were so nice while observing them automatically energy shield the car from the dirt and thieves.

Inside H.Q., Deputy Chief Siv Kratos was examining the daily work logs when his secure tablet notified him of an incoming encrypted text. “I’ve sent new atlas data of the incoming. Are there any new targets to investigate?” Siv was pleased to have the intelligence. “I am mostly concerned with those that are a threat to the quality of life here. The Dacian intelligence was good. No further targets as of yet. Thx.”

A drop of blood landed on the cement basement floor. Draul’s head hung loose as he attempted to gain all the strength he could. His hands bound behind him, his feet were strapped to the chair. Ramses stood relaxed a few feet away with his sleeves rolled up revealing his forearms. Standing next to him was a hooded person wearing some sort of long black trench coat with an elongated nose and chin which was nearly all one could see of his face. The dimly lit room had a thickness in the atmosphere and reeked of sweat.

Ramses spoke with a deep base, "Where are our friends? Why are you abducting our friends? You people don't like to play within the rules, eh?" Draul hoarsely whispered, "You're not real, and I won't say anything about it." Ramses' nostrils flared slightly. "You're going to have a lot more than a bloody nose if you don't tell us what we want to know. You see Anurah over here can make your life a bit more than 'uncomfortable'." Draul sneered slightly and said nothing.

Ramses turned to Anurah, "Let's give our friend a taste, shall we? I'll show you something 'real', moron." Anurah lifted his hands and circled them towards Draul. In one hand Anurah had some sort of small scepter. Within moments scarab beetles by the thousands began swarming from all directions towards the prisoner who immediately began screaming. Ramses smirked a snarl then said, "And they haven't even touched you yet!" Within moments the beetles were smothering his entire body along with the chair while Draul screamed. Anurah again lifted his arms in a circular motion and the beetles vanished.

Briefly looking at Ramses, Anurah again lifted his scepter. With the other hand thrust a small ball of thread into the air. Suddenly the atmosphere in the room became so thick it was nearly liquid. Ramses jerked and quickly adjusted while Draul slightly choked and shifted being clearly caught off guard by the change. The ball of thread slowed and suddenly burst into a luminous ball. The space around the light began stretch until it became clear that it was some sort of portal to somewhere or something.

Ramses smiled with dominant confidence, "We can abduct you as well. You have no idea what kind of amazing little places we can send you. Do you care to discover how real the little virtual-scape is on the other end of that portal?" Sarcastically continuing, "You may find it to be a little piece of heaven."

Reaching into his pocket, Ramses revealed a small eye dropper with some neon green liquid in it. Ramses walked closer to Draul who was jerkily trying to find a way to avert the approaching encounter with Ramses. "This will sting a bit." Gripping Draul's head, Ramses jerked it back causing a small snapping noise. Anurah reached for the eye dropper as Ramses forcefully opened Drauls eyes. Dropping a few drops into each eye, Draul screamed very briefly until he realized it was not all that painful.

"Look! Look all around you!" Ramses roared. Draul apparently could now see a large quantity of various energies in the room. Ramses was extremely knowledgeable of the state of matter known as energy. "Do you know what happens to matter when it gets really hot?" Ramses sneered then scoffed,

"You must have no idea what we are capable of." Surrounding Draul from what he could tell was all sorts of energy forms. Many looked very strange to him. Giant spiders spun webs for some unknown possibly terrible objectives while falcon headed creatures peered into what seemed like his soul. "See the energies in this domain, this world. They don't take kindly to your behavior. We can chase you through hyperspace whenever needed."

Looking intently at Draul, Ramses continues, "You have seen who resides here now that you are not blind to this place. Your friends would probably rather hide that from you." Ramses grabs a chair with a sigh while observing Draul, sweat beading around his head. "I see you'd rather not give us what we want. Anurah, please." Anurah aimed his scepter at Draul and it begun to emit some pulsating light which also made a small crackling noise. Visible microwaves quickly reach Draul, who immediately begins screaming from some unknown effect. Blood again begins to trickle out his nose to the cement while he reels.

Approaching his desk, John could not help noticing the large coffee in the commonly known Starbucks warming cup placed centrally on his light wooden desk with rounded steel supports. Next to the coffee was one of his preferred protein bars a Nike 'Pharrell'. Smirking widely, he scanned the room. Tina looked up at him from her computer and said, "Don't look at me." Then he noticed Rhea with her long flowing blond hair nicely styled and her deep blue eye's beaming at him. "You know. I am glad Kratos decided not to terminate you. You are exceptional, thank you." Rhea, laughed with pleasure. "You know technically, I out rank you so you better watch it."

Looking across his desk, John eyed his partner, Thoth who was likewise scrutinizing John. "Is there a high probability of the theft being linked to our new incoming guests? Them being the friendlies they seem to be," Thoth opened the conversation. Nodding his head with a serious look, John responded. "So it seems. They did actually attempt to take money unlike the incident at Dacian's place. There is no description of course." Thoth chuckled. "Naturally, they hide from sight, or it is simply not in their nature to show themselves. Possibly they have a permanent locked closet complex."

Thoth was finely detailed slightly tanned white male with a very short cut go-tee. His medium cut light brown and uncurled hair bounced effortlessly as he moved his head. His form was thick yet obviously low in body fat covered by a finely tailored grey sports jacket.

John opened his laptop and begun writing a quick outline for his report after sipping his Cappuccino. Meanwhile, Thoth was investigating newly arrived residents. “It is not all that surprising that 80 percent of newly arriving residents are blind.” Thoth mumbles to himself. John wrapped up his report which nicely explained the events in a way that his target audience would understand. “Mark is a new resident, and he is a target. Also, the incident at Dacian’s place was a bit odd, and he was blind.” Thoth still looking at his computer responded. “They did not steal anything from Dacian, we don’t even know what their motives were.” John nodded in agreement.

Thoth looked at John directly then reached one arm forward on the desk. “Why do these guys think they can simply take? Don’t they understand how the system works? They behave more like a criminal raiding party.” John responded, “They seem to typically accuse their victims of this or that, such as not being ‘real’. It seems as though they think they are somehow justified. Other such raiding groups have played within the rules.”

Thoth’s tablet notified him of an incoming call. Thoth chuckled and thought it was funny, Tina calling him from across the office. “Dispatch reports a possible missing persons report. A Rae Osira has been reported as not found and not showing to any of his appointments. I’ll send the address of residency and other available details over. Rae is in my circle of friends, so you better find him!” Thoth frowned at John. “Missing person? Should we send rookie over to verify that he is not simply out of the house on his own accord?” John laughed. “No, I have been looking over the details, and I think we should have a look.”

After dropping the report at Siv Kratos’s office, they proceeded to Rae’s house. Rae lived in a gated luxury home community. Parking in Rae’s oversized sloping driveway, everything seemed uneventful and undisturbed. John and Thoth exited the enforcer issued Ford GT. Rae’s gold concrete house showed no activity other than a lingering police officer as they approached it. They swiftly passed through the police lines and examined the doorway first.

“No sign of forced entry. Perhaps he left his door unlocked while inside?” Thoth quickly zapped.

Whisking inside, they investigated further. Approaching them, Eurus was holding a tablet with notes. "Seems like a robbery, there is nothing of any value here. There is no jewelry in the house and several blank spaces where furniture and wall objects were previously located. Unless, he decided to take his stuff and exit without telling anyone it was theft." John looked at him, "Prints? DNA capable residue?" Eurus sighed. "We're still looking. There are lots of remnants pointing to Rae. No blood or anything." John looked at Thoth, "We're going to interview neighbors within view. Let us know if you find anything interesting."

"Hang on. I am going to check Rae's records real quick and see if there is any reason for him to up and leave on his own accord." John zapped at Thoth while making his way to the car. Following behind him Thoth complimented him. "Good idea. There does not appear to be any struggle here and thus far no actual evidence of anything other than someone took off with all the valuables."

John tapped a bit on his paper-thin tablet. "Ok, get this. Rae, was an independently wealthy technocrat and appeared to have no present financial issues. He has a number of profitable investments primarily in video game developers as well as a few other technology companies. Apparently he has a high level of technical skill by the looks of the resume." Thoth looking at John and breathed a serious sigh. "Let's check with the neighbors."

They swiftly commandeered several police officers directing them like a military operation. "We'll take the house with the friend." John pointed to a nearby house. Thoth smirked and scrutinized the house. "The lagger Falcon? Good thinking. They seem to show up at unique places." They quickly approached the doorway.

Thoth waved at the door alarm. A finely detailed elderly man opened the door. John looked him over with fine detail. "You have a friend. Do you know him?" John pointed at the peregrine falcon. The man lightly chuckled while observing the Falcon. "Fine animals, how can I help you?"

Thoth looked at the gentleman with detailed scrutiny. "We are investigating a possible robbery or disappearance of a Rae Osira. When was the last time you noticed any activity at the residency across the way?" Thoth said while pointing to Rae's place.

"Two days ago, I remember. I thought it was odd. There was an old rusty truck parked in the driveway. It was odd because vehicles of that sort don't frequent around here. Another thing that was very odd, a black cloud of dust or gas was near his house. Very strange, like something in the air. The resident, I am only an acquaintance of, briskly left with another man, the driver." John showed pleasant partial surprise. "Can you advise of the approximate location of the..uh..truck?" Pointing to an area of the driveway the elderly man responded. "It was around there."

"Do you have a description of the man Rae was with?" Thoth continued while lightly rubbing his chin. The elderly man smiled and motioned with his hands while talking. "He was blond short haired and slightly taller than Rae. He was wearing jeans and a white t-shirt. Sorry, I cannot be more specific than that." John smiled warmly glad to have any information. “Thank you very much. You have been a great help.” Turning to return to the crime scene, John briefly noticed that the peregrine was gone. He looked at Thoth. “A black cloud?” Thoth smirked then continued, “Must be our new arrivals.”

Returning to the driveway, they carefully examined it for evidence of any sort. The other officers returned having come up empty. Suddenly, John noticed a small amount of black dust with a tiny bit of tire print. Waving to one of the nearby specialists, John elaborates. “We’ll get this analyzed and find out if there is anything like it in the area. No matter how hard they try there is almost always something to find.” Thoth laughed with enthusiasm while holding his hands confidently at his hips. “I am sort of surprised the elderly man saw the black cloud though.”

John quickly zapped the descriptions to H.Q. and then slipped into the driver seat. Moments after they left the driveway, his tablet announced a response from H.Q. Thoth grabbed his tablet. “They’ve recovered what they think to be the truck. It was abandoned on the side of Iris Road.” John smirked while smoothly navigating and responded. “Let me guess it was stolen and there are zero prints.” Thoth chuckled while returning Johns tablet. “Yep, nothing. They are still going over it, but nothing.” John responded with a sigh shifting his head slightly. “Let’s hope that black material gives us a lead.”

Chapter 6

Friends

Mark rapidly moved his mouse around the screen, occasionally utilizing the keyboard like fingers of light. He was currently designing the Internet interface for the game. He planned to have as much Internet interface as it seemed logical, including trading (even selling) game items. There was an option for the hosting company to '3-D print' objects from the game and send them to players. Suddenly, over the intercom, the receptionist queried, "Mark, you have some visitors. Garrick Nukis and Jeff Horus are here in the lobby. Should I send them in?" Mark replied, "Sure send them on up."

Mark, filled with anticipation, thought, was it Garrick from his dream? He'd never met Garrick in the flesh. Standing at the door was a tall darker-yet-still-white male with short wavy hair. Next to him was another male with slightly elongated slender arms, auburn hair, and dark-green eyes. "That's the usual smile. Garrick, my imaginary friend, has come to life and arrived here across space and time! What's up?" Mark remarked, trying to jest. Garrick laughed. "Yep, I'm that Garrick. Nice to actually meet you while in a waking side of the universe." Mark turned to Jeff and signed the question: "How are you?" Mark had previously met Jeff, and he was a mute who communicated via sign language.

"What has been going down as of late?" Jeff hand signed his question with a smile. Mark suddenly turned serious with a monotone look on his face. "I've had contact with some unusual events. A 'voice' or ghost - I'm not sure what else to call it - tried to talk to me at one of my parties, and some fraudulent charges mysteriously show on my credit card statement. Have you guys had any unusual contact lately?" Mark spoke and signed it at the same time. Garrick looked at him with a serious yet pondering look while reaching toward Mark's tablet. "Can you show me the charges?" Mark swiftly logged in to his bank account. "Here, see the charge descriptions. One of them says 'You're not real.' That is the same thing the voice said. I cannot be certain, yet it seems the same. It may have a connection. Also, another windstorm-like voice nearly assaulted me and confirmed it had something to do with this by claiming it was 'only a sample' of what it might do."

Jeff responded, saying that he had not noticed anything, and even if they tried to talk to him, he probably wouldn't have noticed. Smiling Jeff signed to Mark asking if he checked to verify that he was in fact 'real'. Mark laughed, "Very funny. Perhaps, I am not real? 'L-O-L' The question is what does it mean by real?" Garrick responds, "What isn't real according to them? These strangers have an odd way of thinking so it may be anything. It could be video games you design, they may think you are a character in a dream, your look is fake, etc., etc."

Garrick, in deep contemplation, continued, "I have had contact with someone, come to think of it. I notice some odd mnemonics of various blind people, listening and talk suggestively when someone said some strange things like 'Why so quiet?' I sort of ignored it and mumbled to myself that something seemed crazy. Then suddenly, a strange dog suddenly started barking ferociously at me." Mark smirked sarcastically. "Now now, calling them crazy! You angered some strange dog! 'L-O-L' " Then he continued with a friendly smile, "Yeah, yeah. I understand you. Your experience seems similar to mine. It sort of makes me feel like I am going crazy. Whatever 'it' is; it seems to get mad. It is more like a ghost or spirit and doesn't quite know what to make of us. It also cannot read us very well. Perhaps we can take advantage of the reading difficulty it seems to have."

Mark considered things a bit and then said, "What we need to do is make a silent zone somewhere such as our bedrooms, then make sure that we make no noise at all when there. Put a silencer on it then lock and load. If we need to talk, we can sign it. When we talk via phone, we text it rather than speak so they will not know what we are saying." Garrick, smiling, responded, "Perfect. Now we need to somehow locate the guys who are plotting this siege of sorts. I have a feeling they may attempt to steal from you/us again." Mark adjusted himself in his chair and took a sip of his energy drink—at which point, he turned and looked at the guys. "Do you guys know any blind people? It only makes sense that they are blind. Of course, it does not rule out sight. They may and probably have seeing friends. Do you know anyone that could be a lead on this? There must be a reason they picked us."

Garrick smirked. "Who knows why? Perhaps we have valuables, and they think there is some way to get to them. Isn't that the most common reason thieves pick their victims?" Mark nodded. "Right. Well, I'm not ruling out anything. For now, that is as good a reason as any. We are different peas in different pods, perhaps this how they try to push around the 'other guys'?" Jeff signed a response to that. "That's what I'm thinking.

If that is true, they are a gang of sorts, probably with a leader. First thing we need to do is find something about them and secure ourselves against attacks, possibly teach people who may be spying for them a lesson." Mark smiled in agreement while examining his hand. "We need to find any moles. Pay special attention to anything that would suggest it."

Later, Mark finally made his way to his bed, like diving into a very comfortable pool. Shifting into the usual dream state, Mark found himself with his arms holding Tia's nude skin close. Tia's face and hands were smothering him; he had already penetrated her. She bounced repeatedly for what seemed like a long time before they retired to a comfortable relaxed position.

Suddenly, the landscape changed, and Mark found himself near the location he previously had been. It was obviously some sort of burial ground that apparently had a constant lightning storm and was a home to various crows. The crows again made the same eerie announcements of his presence.

Mark decided it was time to find out what this place was. He pulled out the key and placed it in the dream catcher. Moments later, lightning zapped repeatedly immediately in front of him, causing Mark to suddenly and slightly stumble backward a bit, unsure of the safety. The crows flew toward a distant location of the stormy region. A short distance away, a mist of dark and luminous particles seemingly came out of the air. The mist combined to form a sitting elderly Indian. Drums began to beat, and the crows returned to the vicinity. Mark was like, "Wow, smooth!"

The Indian began to speak. "The one that seeks you is a dark one. He has issues with your silent sun." Mark smiled confidently. "Who are you?" The Indian smiled yet remained serious, and in a sort of methodical manner, responded, "I am Elder of Beyond, spirit of nature's winds." Mark, to the point, asked, "Are you human?" The Indian responded, "I am a spirit of nature, not humanity. You may find a way to utilize the dark one's blind belief. It is possible to catch them off guard if you are true. As a matter of opinion you can entrap them. We will also attempt to find them out." With that, the entire burial ground vanished.

Mark opened his eyes immediately to a sunlit room. So these were not the odd "voices" that were trying to steal from him then. He'd have to keep looking. Even though it was merely a dream, Mark thought it had really smooth effects.

Mark quickly moved to the edge of his bed and looked around his partially furnished room. He was actually immediately wide awake with a sense of inner satisfaction, as usual. "This place still needs some furnishing," he muttered to himself. The "need" was evident by the clothing strewn around the floor and the solitary bed stand. The rest of the house was also lightly furnished.

The nice thing about being an independent contractor was that he could simply decide he had to go do something for the day and do it. After quick preparation, Mark smoothly strolled toward his Acura in his shimmering dress shirt and pants. Mark's dress shirt was a dark blue with a pattern of shiny lines. It was quite warm today, and Mark did not even notice. Navigating his long trench coat, he positioned himself in the driver's seat of the car.

Mark visited several furniture stores yet was rather disappointed. He seemed to have trouble locating the precise style and quality he was looking for. Mark located a furniture store, which he suspected would be more of the same—a local store called Jack's Furniture. After meandering in, Mark immediately noticed some incredible choices that stood out from a large portion of the store. "That collection just came in yesterday. You like it?" The salesman beckoned to Mark. Mark was a bit suspicious as to why a place like this would carry such obviously expensive furniture that looked a little unlike the rest of the store, yet he disregarded it, feeling others must have a sense of style as well.

Mark quickly selected some of the pieces, which were made of material such as velvet, brass, glass, stone, and even concrete. The prices were very reasonable for such pieces, causing Mark to carefully examine them. However, he found them to be entirely of exceptional quality, and seemingly built to last, possibly longer than a human's life span. The furniture was scheduled for delivery later that day, and Mark made his way toward a nearby restaurant for lunch.

The restaurant of choice was in the nearby megalithic shopping mall. Mark opened the larger-than-life all-glass door at the front of the main, mostly concrete, entrance and made his way toward the specialty sandwich shop. Immediately, he noticed a young female he had briefly met at his party.

Her brown hair was long enough to reach her shoulders, complementing her deep-green eyes and full lips. She was reasonably tall with smooth flowing curves teasingly partially exposed by her relaxed white top and short pastel-green skirt. Standing and looking around, she noticed him and smiled a sort of flirty smirk. Mark swiftly approached, holding his hands in a partial grip of the air, his index finger pointed slightly while his arms and legs moved in perfect symphony with his head angled in a slightly aloof state. Mark partially spun toward her and slightly cocked his head with a smirk. "Mairis, right?" She smiled with seemingly internal satisfaction at the acknowledgement. "Yeah, that's me. You're Mark, from the party?" Mark smiled in response. "That's me. Did you like the party?" Her body movement spoke volumes as she quickly said, "Oh yeah, it was hot." Mark smirked at that. "Did you have a phone number? Perhaps we could rendezvous sometime?" Mairis very slightly jumped and smiled as she wrote her number. "Sure, that seems like fun. Call me." Mark closed it at that and continued to his lunch objective.

Reaching the sandwich shop, Mark briefly examined the menu. The waitress approached Mark and seductively greeted him, "Hi, Mark. How can I help you?" He looked at her soft flowing brown hair as it partially covered her smooth skin, which exposed a solitary beauty mark. Mark non-aggressively yet playfully responded, "Hello, Kara, how are you? Where is Rae?" Kara looked at him and responded with a slightly lower tone, "You didn't know? Rae is a missing person. He suddenly disappeared along with most of his valuables." Mark turned serious. "Ah, that—uh, is unfortunate. Do you miss him now that he is missing? I'll bet you miss his…uh, valuables. I'll take the usual." With that, she laughed and whisked away.

Mark's tablet alerted him that he had a text, and he quickly examined it. It was Garrick, of course. "I am revisiting the location previously spoke of and had contact with the blind. I'll let you know what I find." Mark thought about that himself. Perhaps he could look around the house. Until this point, he had primarily assumed they were visiting his house.

Mark admired the melting drip of cheese smothering the thick cuts of roast beef in the lightly toasted sandwich bread on the plate Kara was delivering. "Kara, the way you handle the plate suggests it may be magnetically attracted to you or you are handling it via quantum entanglement," Mark compliments while flicking his right hand her direction. Sitting forward Mark goes on, "Why do you continue to work here? I am sure Rae could find something for you to do." Smiling assuredly Kara retorts, "I only work here part time. I like this place and job. I get to see my friends such as yourself. My connections are important to me even the ones who respond via quantum mechanics."

"Ah…I spent my day primarily furniture matching until I came upon Jack's," Mark casually reported. Kara's eyes lit up and slightly squinted as she responded, "You discovered Jack's! Yea, that place has a sort of psychic quality to it. I am assuming you found something suitable then." Mark smirked at that and responded, "That I did, that I did."

After a full day of furnishing his house orientated for good energy flow, Mark found his way to his bed. Having looked all around the house and yard, he could find nothing to suggest that the strangers were not simply "visitors." He had examined his yard, even the trees and shrubbery. There was nothing unusual, and they looked similar to his neighbors'. He lay on his bed, and his mind meandered, shifting into the state of sleep. Mark found himself sitting on a couch, watching television.

Channel 88 news was on, displaying an incident at a mall. Everything was very similar yet different, and there was no Channel 88 in his waking version. It was still most certainly Olympus. Mark wasn't sure at this point, yet if he had to guess, it was either simply a dreamscape or he had leaped into an alternate thread in the multiverse. Having been here a few time, he had scrutinized what little he could before.

Standing up he meandered into the dining room. The decor was a mix of stars/astrology, modern sophistication, and Egyptian hieroglyph. In the corner was a large terrarium with various lizards. Tia was standing in the kitchen, cooking breakfast. "Nice of you to show." Mark, smirking, fired back, "Hi, yeah. I still retain the right to inter-fishbowl travel." Tia looked him directly in the eyes; her deep-green eyes seemed to flow like currents in the sun. Suddenly, she returned to her breakfast and attempted to fix it. "Uuh."

Mark examined the scene a bit more. He noticed a fresh fruit bowl lay resting in the center of the kitchen counter with vibrant exceptionally fresh and lacking blemish. The mango seemed perfect along with the kiwi, grapes, limes, oranges and dates.

Tina reached for the fruit; above the fruit bowl were some black cherries hanging from the cabinet. The cherries seemed to have a sort of black mist around it. Mark suddenly realized that she was reaching for the bowl because one of the cherries was falling toward the fruit bowl. He reached out with swift lightning fast reflexes. Unfortunately, lightning speed was not enough and neither did Tina catch it. The cherry landed on the dates.

The entire fruit bowl faded from vibrant to black, dead and rotten. A slight anomaly or clear cloud seemed to float away from the fruit as if its spirit was leaving. He was shocked by how rapid the decay occurred, it seemed extremely unnatural.

Looking at Tina she winced in pain. Grasping her stomach she stumbled to the floor. Tears swelled in her eyes as they rolled. Mark immediately attempted to console her. She muttered, "She's dead." Mark was surprised that he seemed unaffected. It was like some event was effecting her via quantum entanglement. Glancing up at the remaining cherries he thought to himself, "Now to immunize the environment to the remnants before they ruin anything else."

Chapter 7

The New Contract

Mark was sitting in front of his computer; he was considering the orientation of one of the symbol puzzles he had previously made. There was a knock on the door, and he turned to face it. "Hi, Mark. How is it?" Ben said. Ben was his current contractor, and Mark was aware that his contract was coming to an end. "Smooth as silk, other than the odd thieves," Mark sharply responded with confidence. "As you know, your contract will be up next month, and I said I would try to find you another contract spot. The good news is, I think I have something. The bad news is, it will not be here with us, and there are not a lot of other choices. In fact, if you don't want the contract, I don't think I'll have anything for you. You'd be on your own," Ben elaborated with a sigh.

That wasn't like Ben; something seemed wrong. Mark pondered that. "Well, what is it?" Ben labored to smile. "A new voice-activated space research program. It sounds fairly interesting, but that is all I have right now." Mark laughs. "Well, it does seem sort of interesting. If that is my only option, sounds like I'll probably skill and destroy it." Ben finally laughed. "Okay, I'll set up an interview and see what they try for."

Mark's tablet announced that he had a text, and Mark picked it up. "No go on the blind people connection. No trace of them." Mark returned, "NP. Let me know if there is anything else." Mark quickly dialed Mairis. "You want to do something tonight, say 5:30?" Mairis responded positively, "Sure." Mark turned toward the computer; he had a few days to finish this and enough work for about one day. Fortunately for him, his contract gave him two months' pay at the end. If he picked up a contract right away, he would actually have extra money.

Mark swiftly grabbed his jacket and made for his Acura. Reaching for the ignition of his car Mark was suddenly aware that someone was nearby. Slowly, he lifted his head and stealthily scanned the area when suddenly a light knock on the window. It was Mairis. Mark sighed with relief as he opened the door. “You came here to my work parking lot? I was going to pick you up.” Mairis chuckled and moved into a comfortable position resting on the exterior of Marks car. “It’s easier that way. This way I have my car with me. Can we drop it at your place?”

“Sure, my place is fine. I was looking forward to seeing your place.” Mark zapped back while still processing everything. Is she hiding something, or is she simply planning to stay at my place? Mark wondered. “There will be a time for that. I hope that is acceptable.” Mairis brushed herself off nonchalantly. Mark nodded and gestured to the effect of ‘no problem’.

After dropping Mairis’ car, they made their way to the nearby theater. Parking the car, Mark looked at Mairis. “You like movies don’t you?” Turning and looking him directly in his shimmering eyes. “Yes, yes. Let’s watch a movie.” Quickly reviewing the movie list he mumbles, “Mandelbrot Jumper, States of Matter, The Pattern Repeaters, White Nose Plague, Masters of Khi, Acuteness of Vision, Kumonosu.” Mark then continues, “Any preferences? I am sort of leaning towards Masters of Khi.”

Leisurely strolling toward the theater, Mark scrutinized the theater. It was clearly one of Ramses’ designs with many pathways leading to several megalithic central points in a web-like pattern. Nearly, everything was concrete, colossal and sort of like a connected net as opposed to one enormous building. It was not actually a single building, yet displayed the idea that they were connected while some nearby buildings clearly not connected. The style was perfect for the theater which always had several shows playing.

Admiring an abstract wall art piece Mark recently installed, Mairis showed genuine interest, clearly smothering the canvas's details. Mark moved close and, in a low tone, said, "You like it? It seems to sort of extend from the wall into a possible other realm somewhere in its depths, doesn't it?"

Mairis turned toward Mark. "I see that." Mark reached around her head, touching her cheek. He guided her face toward his mouth and immediately began to explore her mouth, among other parts. Mairis immediately appeared to sort of melt in his embrace, and all she could think was "smooth." Turning her back toward the wall, she slightly stumbled backward. Mark immediately responded by shifting toward the wall where she rested against it. She tugged on Mark's torso area.

After a short while of exploring the wall and several dimensions of each other's body, Mark pushed her in the direction of his giant bed. Mairis responded quickly with exuberance, pushing Mark onto the large bed while a few drops of sweat made its way toward the lower portion of her chin.

Standing in the doorway, Mark partially entered the room where Ben was clicking away on his computer. Looking up, Ben queried in a matter-of-fact way, "How can I help you?" Mark seriously responded with a slightly inquisitive tone, "Do you have the company name? The one with my future contract?" Ben positively responded, "Sure, Applied Dynamics. I'll e-mail you the address so you can do some preliminary research." Mark smirked assuredly. "Thanks, Ben. Thanks a lot for everything over the years." Mark wanted to try and make sure he had a friend to return to after this.

Returning to his desk, Mark located the Applied Dynamics Web site. A very basic Web site, it seemed as though it was a bit of a cookie-cutter-made site. Mark quickly texted Garrick, "Can you meet at the Cyberpad? How soon can you guys be there?" Cyberpad was a hot spot for Internet, LAN games, energy drinks, and coffee—among other things. After a few moments, Mark had his response. "NP. I'm already there. When will you show?" With that, Mark grabbed his keys and trench coat while making for the door, all in one smooth stroke.

The solitary waiter/bus girl dropped off several twenty-four-ounce energy beverages while making seductive eye contact with Garrick. "You're awwe-some sizzles, thx. When you want to get off, you can linger with us. Drop your number, and I'll be in contact." Garrick responded to her eye contact with a smirk. Looking down at the table, she responded in a matter-of-fact way, "I work late tonight. Here's my number, though." Mark chuckled; she already had it ready. What was her plan?

The decor of the Cyberpad was futuristic as anything, yet Mark could see slight undertones of a time before the computer. Everything had smooth lines and curves, rarely any excessive frill yet with a few appealing patterns. The cybernetic wall art was very interesting and painted directly onto the walls in bright vivid colors mixed with dark ones. The arms on the low chairs and couches had a sharp edge that swooped in a curved manner directly into the chair, which appeared to be a single-piece assembly. The table appeared as though it might be vortex-inspired while the automatic glass sliding doors had curved corners. Looking up, the ceiling was farther than ten feet. A giant bronzed falcon, purposely done with smooth surfaces rather than fluffy detail, was suspended in midair.

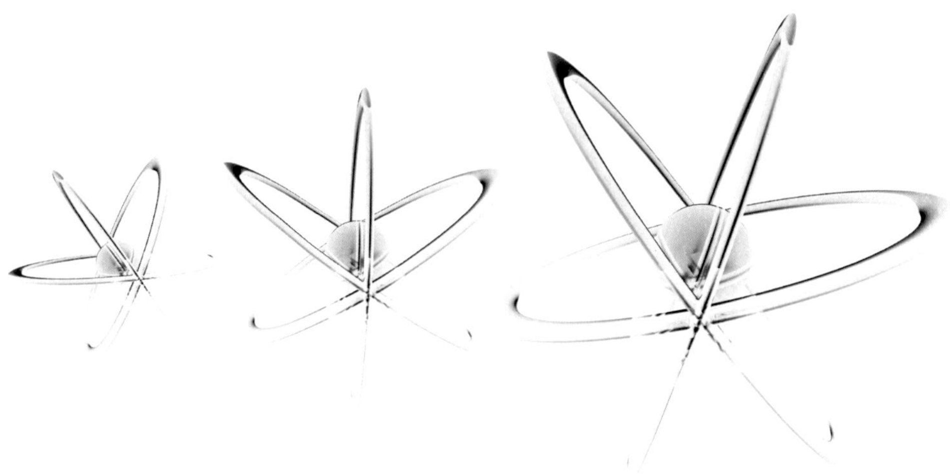

All three of them had their tablets out, and Garrick had his laptop as well. Mark displayed his tablet browser on the table, which had a display enabled surface. "How's my friend from across space-time? Did you search the news for activity with blind people? I am thinking of repeating patterns that link to our..uh.. interesting intruders." Garrick responded in a slightly negative tone while playing with his short yet wavy hair, "You said they claimed that the police would not find anything, so chances are it will be hard to detect. I did look a bit, though, and did not find anything unusual. Just because a person is blind does not make them part of the gang that is harassing you." Mark concurred completely, "Yes, that is true. Can we look again real quick? What about that Dacian Wilson who was robbed a while back? Garrick, see what you can find about Applied Dynamics. Who is in charge, who owns it, etc. Jeff, help me check out Dacian and anything else we can find." Garrick muttered, "Applied Dynamics, why them?" Mark looked at him. "That is my next contract, my only option, and I am quite suspicious of them."

With that, they pursued the targets when Mark's tablet alerted him of a call. In a smooth overly friendly tone, Mark answered, "How are you? Did you do that to your hair? It's black." Mairis laughs seductively in a way, suggesting an "if you only knew" tone, lightly touching her face and mouth. "Yes, I did a makeover. Where are you? What are you doing tonight?" Mark was thinking "nice" then smirked and said, "We are at the Cyberpad. Why don't you drop and linger?" Mairis smiled, her full lips forming an assured pout. "I'll do that, see you in a bit."

Mark returned to his browsing. He had located Dacian and attempted a quick look at anything he could find, even doing a two-credit address search. He looked at Garrick. "Find anything?" Garrick looked at him studiously then began, "Applied Dynamics is a small to medium company that is funded and owned by an independent yet-to-be-determined investor. The CEO goes by Chris Vocal who is presently worth five million, owning a few homes. Get this, the CFO is a blind person by the name of John Cords, and everything must be translated into braille for him. Dacian Wilson, the guy you are looking up, is a managing director at the local manufacturing facility. Did you get his address?" Mark nodded. "Yes. Dacian is also blind." Garrick continued, "Applied Dynamics designs and develops, as far as I can tell, space-air-sea equipment for all sorts of purposes. Your new contract may be with people that are associated with the crazy voices." They continued for a bit on that topic.

Turning toward the door, Mark noticed Mairis approaching. Her long now-black locks of shiny hair moved in a slightly yet smooth-flowing fashion while her short black dress hugged her curves, allowing a little imagination as she streamed toward them. As she got closer, Mark could not help but recognize similarity to Tia. Mark smiled. "Mairis, you're here!" Mairis beamed. "Hi, do, what is happening on the flip side?" Mark quickly signed a translation for Jeff even though Jeff usually could read lips. Garrick smiled. "Just doing a bit of research hopefully on our harassers." Mairis immediately sat down as if she was nearly in the same physical spot as Mark, gripping him while she removed her white and light green leather jacket to further reveal her nice little black dress.

Mairis's eyes were slightly raccoon-like by her eyeliner, yet she wore only light amounts of makeup, including shimmering lavender lipstick, complementing her plump, full lips. Her feet were covered by heelless black leather shoes that sort of wrapped around her feet, making them look like a second skin, with a neon-green atomic symbol on the side. Mark quickly jabbed, "You like the Cyberpad, Mairis?" Mairis smiled warmly as she pulled out her minitablet. "Absolutely, it sizzles." Jeff quickly started signing at Mark. Mark chuckled, "He likes your tab. Is it the one with projector?" Mairis laughed loftily. "Yes, I just upgraded it. It's so awesome."

Mark turned to Garrick and continued, "Well, there is nothing wrong/deviant about being blind in and of itself. The question is do they have anything to do with the harassment? Jeff, look up John Cords and Chris Vocal. It is a bit odd that these people have very limited history available. See if you find anything further. Garrick, don't you think the Applied Dynamics Web site is a bit cookie-cutterish?"

Garrick swiftly moved his hand around his tablet screen. "Yeah, most certainly. Nothing special about it, not really any company art other than the logo." Mark did a trace route on the Web address then handed Garrick half of the nodes on the list directly to his tablet. "Check those out, I'll check these." After a few moments, Garrick stated in a matter-of-fact tone, "This node list goes out of state . . . to California." Mark looked at him. "Yeah, it's a Web hosting service, a cheap one too . . . matching the Web site. They don't even design their own Web site, much less host and manage their own Web site. All that Internet technology too complicated for them?" They all laughed at that, and Mark continued, "Hyperspace probably messing with their bat senses." They continued laughing for a bit.

"It is possible that they are all a front for something else. The history seems very limited like they just showed up and made a few things up or something." Garrick then looked at Jeff. "We should get going. I need to work on the morrow." Jeff signed back, "That's good, I should get home as well. I have some video games that need completing." Mark turned to Jeff. "What do you do, for work?" Jeff signed back, smirking like he owned it, "I test video games." Mark sat back, opening his mouth, his whole body sort of chuckling. "Ohhhh, that is smooth. What a tough job that must be. Is it awesome?" Jeff's whole body was nodding yes as he spelled out Y-E-S. Mairis laughed. "I'm so envious." Mark turned to Mairis. "You want to 'hit-it' to my place?" She looked at him and locked lips then mumbled, "The plan I was hoping for." Mark turned toward Garrick and Jeff. "Okay, dos, we'll 'check-it' later."

Sitting at his nice modern stone dining table, Mark had an excellent view of his deck and yard. He scanned the yard and quickly noticed that the landscape seemed a bit different than a few weeks ago. Rising from his seat, he grabbed his cappuccino and walked to the deck to take a closer look, all in one smooth motion.

Turning as he walked, he noticed Mairis cooking breakfast. She looked nearly identical to Tia. He commented to himself that since her makeover, she was so similar to Tia; he could have sworn it actually was Tia. He had known Tia for years in his dreams and thought he knew Tia pretty well. Mairis looked directly at Mark as he observed her. "Did you notice my new car? Do you like it?" Mark, now standing at the glass doors to the deck, smiled. "Ah, it's a classic. The 1997 Lotus Esprit. Yeah, it sizzles." Mairis smirked with a nearly lottery-winning-bad-girl look as a solitary teardrop streamed toward her chin. "I had to sign my life away to get it, but it is most certainly worth every penny thus far."

Mark looked out the windows to his yard, returning to his previous objective. The trees were noticeably different. Even the shrubs and grass were different. Mark quickly scanned his neighbor's yard, which still appeared the same, to assure himself that he wasn't delusional. The grass looked much softer and velvety now.

The trees and shrubbery noticeably swooped in smooth curves, lines, and sharp edges. Mairis, still tending to the eggs and bacon continued, "I am going to get a carbon fiber body kit and hood when I can muster up the monies. Don't you think that would look hot?" Mark smirked while observing his yard. "Good idea. I do that to all my cars." Mark scanned his neighbor's shrubbery again, which looked prickly and rough despite being nicely cut and detailed.

Mairis looked up at him and said, "I really like how you have designed your domain here. The decor has a really extraordinary aesthetics." Mark, sipping his coffee, looked at her and smirked. "Yeah, it sizzles. I am pleased you find it appealing. Obviously, you have good taste—much like myself. One reason I like you." Stepping back with a slight of thoughtfulness, she said, "You'll have to help me design and assemble my domain some time. I would love that!" Suddenly noticing that the atmosphere in the room seemed warm and inviting with a thick-like energy, Mark shifted his eyes then responded, "Absolutely, we can do that. That seems like it would be a blast!"

Mark turned toward the dinette table and sat where Mairis had placed his plate. Contemplating what he had just observed, he looked around his the room. Finally, he thought to himself, it's as if the outside is now reflecting my style here on the inside, awesome. It did seem to look like his own style had affected every corner of his yard. Reaching into his pocket, Mark pulled some cash out of his wallet and placed it near Mairis then whispered, "Body kit and hood." Mairis slightly leaped and smiled. "Thank you so much. You are awesome." Calming down a bit, she took a bite of food while seemingly examining the other side of the room. "I really like your dreams."

Mairis' tablet announced an incoming call to which she answered briskly. "Hello?" It was Officer John Thomas who immediately responded, "I wanted you to know that Tina has been reported missing. She did not show up for work and was not found at her apartment. We will be investigating it shortly." Mairis' face turned pale, "Oh, my—." Then she turned silent. Mark inquisitively quickly finished a bite and queried, "What is it?" "Tina is not to be found and was reported missing."

Mark intently examined the screens of his computer; he had been cleaning up his files and codes all day. He figured he could complete the project today if he really wanted to. Ben interrupted by slightly clearing his throat. Turning his head, Mark quickly spun to face Ben. "Applied Dynamics apparently does not need an interview. I guess that's good. In fact, I already have a contract," Ben spelled out, sort of partially upbeat, as he placed a thick stack of stapled paper on the desk. Mark appeared slightly unsure while trying to analyze Ben's position on this, at the same time finding Applied Dynamics fairly predictable. Mark responded, "Right, naturally." Ben continued, "If you agree, sign and return it to me. I'll advise you of where and when after that. Hope everything works out."

Mark completed his work for the day and cleaned up most of the project. Mark reviewed the contract and signed it. Placing his Vision ball pen's cap on the light-gray fine pen, Mark returned the pen to his pocket while contemplating the future of this contract. Paging Ben's phone, Mark advised Ben, "I signed it. Where is Tink, by the way?" Ben responded with positivity, "Tink is already at the new contract site. The same one you are going to. It'll be a different department, yet he is there." Mark dropped the contract at Ben's office before locating the keys of his Acura.

Chapter 8

Meet the new contractor

The automatic garage door was closing behind him as Mark relocated his leather trench coat, enabling a smooth exit of the vehicle. His Acura TLX was gleaming and shining with some very small dusty smudges. Mark had it detailed and washed only a few days ago. The smell of wood and dust wisped around him while he exited into the house.

The sunny clear blue skies emanated through the large glass windows while Mark turned on his entertainment system. Reaching for his espresso maker, he quickly started a cup. Mark then turned and tossed some cubed filet mignon, onions, and pepper in a frying pan. Suddenly, the doorbell announced a guest. Mark swiftly maneuvered to the front door.

"Hello, my dear friend, and how are you?" Mark gleefully acknowledged. Standing at the door, resting his primary weight on one leg, Ramses was wearing a shimmering black vinyl jacket with neon-green stripes, a black pinstriped pair of shimmering dress pants, and a shiny green rayon top, having a brass zipper partially unzipped. Ramses removed his designer sunglasses and said, "How is it, my friend!" Mark, still ecstatic, said, "Come in. Do you want some filet tips?" They quickly relocated to the den-and-kitchen area where the filet cubes were still sizzling.

Mark finished the mini filet wraps and brought them to the table. "Nice yard! Why does yours look so different from all the neighbors'?" Ramses positively queried. "Well, you know it's my magic essence," Mark responded, laughing. Grabbing a tip, Ramses moved to the large foyer area. "I like the lavish decor you've applied. That is a nice piece. Where did you get that?" Mark meandered along. "Oh, that is a piece that I hold captive as a loan guarantee. It is my collateral." Ramses chuckled. "Now, you're a lender and a loan shark, what's next, a bank?" The smooth lines on Ramses' face did not make him appear old. His skin folded in a way that made his face look chiseled and refined, like a block of stone come to life. "A little sharking is always fun, not sure I will go as far as becoming a bank. That requires a lot more focus on things I currently employ my bank to do," Mark responded swiftly while still exposing a slight laugh. "Smart move with the collateral. I've done a bit of loan sharking myself and that is not the only way the sharks roll," Ramses said, with one hand at his side while the other one following his close inspection of the art piece.

Ramses looked at Mark somberly. "My house was burglarized last night. Unfortunately, I was more concerned with the safety of my person while I was out." Chuckling a bit, he continued, "I had no TV, so I came over here to bother you!" Mark looked at him seriously. "Really, any idea who did it?" Ramses' eyes looked to the side then down. "No, they left some weird message on my answering machine in some low raspy whisper-like tone that said something like 'We took what we wanted.' I figured they disguised the voice." Mark then seriously responded, "They might have something to do with the people who tried to rob me. Hopefully, the police will catch on to that." They played some billiards before parting for the evening.

Mark found his way to his silky bed after a brief hot soak. Stopping, he drifted off to the state of mind known as sleep where he found himself on a gigantic walking street during a nice sunny day. The cloudless sky made it feel like there were vast amounts of space available for exploring. Mark suddenly pushed with his legs and leaped into the sky, soaring. As he began to lose a bit of momentum, he again pushed with his hips. Despite the fact that there was only air beneath his legs, he would again leap and soar. Mark could easily control his movement by shifting left or right. Mark soared through the sky a brief while in this manner when an in-flight falcon suddenly maneuvered to his immediate vicinity. It soared next to him and showed him unusual curiosity.

An odd feeling came over Mark, like something was wrong. Looking down, there was a walkway, some beachside houses, and a dark jungle. In the distance a mountain that looked oddly similar to Mount Zurich. Mark decided to take a look since his senses suggested there was something that he knew down there. Landing, Mark looked around. The sandy beach lacked people, yet there were houses. The atmosphere was warm and inviting until the deep dark jungle. Mark had odd sensations as though dangerous things were transpiring. Mark thought, why don't they come out to the beach where it is warm and inviting? He concluded that exposure wasn't the plan. They might be afraid of him and were trying to project fear.

Suddenly, Mark grasped who the person was that may be having an issue. It was Isis, the girl he had met at the party. She might be here somewhere, according to his senses. Mark knelt down and placed his hand out toward the ground. A large spider emerged from under his shirt sleeve. Mark instructed it, "Go and locate Isis." Mark made a brief sweep of the area then decided to visit her place instead. Suddenly the Falcon swept down picked up the spider that appeared to be awaiting the bird on the ground. Mark turned and leaped in the air to visit Isis place, when suddenly, there was a loud noise.

Mark opened his eyes to the usual ceiling patterns and reached for the "noise" that was, in fact, his alarm. After a brief morning preparation, Mark made his way for his garage. Today was Mark's first day and orientation at Applied Dynamics. Here, he would finally see their faces. While Mark's car braced the curves with ease, Mark wondered about Tink. He would have been on-site for a few days and would be a good person to have a nice nonsuspicious conversation with.

He was greeted at the door. "Are you Mark Khiop? It'll be only a moment. Dek will be right out." The gleaming large white desk greeted him in a reception area, with slightly excessive sprawling patterns on the walls, flowing harmoniously with large gold plates announcing results of some sort or another. Mark sat down in an elaborately patterned red chair with gold trim next to a large yet trimmed bamboo plant. "Mark? Hi, I am Dek Plator, team supervisor for the Stinger project. We'll have a briefing in my office, and then I'll have Jaul show you around."

"Welcome to Applied Dynamics. We work on projects for air, space, and sea exploration and activity. For the most part, we help develop the tools and software to assist with proper exploration so as to not expose our fine citizens to the unknown," Dek elaborated in his opening statement. Dek was tapping his pen on his elaborately patterned large dark blackened wood desk. Dek's black hair was so short; it would not move yet matched well with his dark deep-seated eyes and large bushy eyebrows. Dek had a bright-red pocket square in his otherwise all-black ensemble of sports jacket, slacks, and tie. His bright-white shirt matched well with his untanned white yet not-quite-pale skin. Everything in the room looked fairly old world with elaborate waves and frills, yet it was more of an intentional styling than actual.

Mark smiled, purposely providing a look of anticipation, then said, "Thank you, sir. Do you have more specifics on what I will be doing?" Dek showed a slight unsure look in his eyes, yet everything else reeked with an air of confidence and anticipation. Looking at Mark directly, he responded, "Well, I was planning on having you assist with the program positioning of the sonar and sensory for detection. Does that seem like something you can do?" Dek queried. The edges of Dek's mouth jittered slightly on his oily and slightly moist skin, exposing a sense of anticipation for Mark's response. Mark, confident in such a task, considered this as a way to get some inside information. "Absolutely, I think I will like that task. Thank you." Dek assuredly responded, "Great! Let's have Jaul show you around." Pressing a button on his phone, he said, "Jaul, can you show Mark around?"

Jaul walked into the doorway, "Mr. Khiop? Shall we?" Mark smirked at the reference to his family name. "Call me Mark. Yes, let's do this." They immediately made their way through the hallway. Jaul looked at him directly in the eye. "Most of the facilities are actually on a need-to-know basis, but I'll give you the overview and show you your coworkers on the team." Jaul was very slender and lanky. His long arms and torso were clothed with blue striped dress shirt, sleeves folded up at the ends. The shirt was equipped with a few pens in the pocket, a top button undone, and no tie.

Mark inquisitively looked at Jaul. "A coworker came to work here as well. Perhaps you know him? His nick was Tink, and his legal name was Thisis." Jaul smirked. "Yeah, I know where he is. He is on a different team, however. After the tour, I'll take you to him." Jaul breezed around, introducing Mark.

Jaul gently pushed an already partially opened door exposing a neat desk and office area. Sitting in a mesh chair behind a desk facing them and staring intently at a large flat panel screen was a neatly kept male. "This is Larkul. He is an engineer and works on design of the actual sensors." Jaul interrupted the moment with a slight lofty sense of humor. Looking up Larkul jabbed, "Cold facts of what is there. This isn't a video game invention where we render the landscape to our liking." Larkul had deep dark inset eyes, dark brown hair and a slightly pale complexion.

Reaching beneath his thick glasses Larkul rubbed his eyes then greeted them. "Hello, how are you?" Jaul then continued. "Larkul, this is Mark. He is another engineer and he will be working in schematics." Larkul managed a smile with a chuckle that moved his head yet not much of his body. "Nice to meet you Mark. While this isn't exactly a quiet place to work it is a nice place to work." Jaul swiftly exited the room while thanking Larkul.

Walking slowly past offices with windowed walls, Jaul pointed at the people inside. "That is Tamvis. He is also a sensor engineer, a junior one. Any questions should go to Larkul." Moving swiftly he pointed to another windowed office. "There is Tarsus. He is also in schematics, he is busy right now yet you might want to talk to him if there are any issues with general layout."

Breezing on, Jaul opened one of the doors quietly. On the right and behind a desk was a male with a dark complexion. Deep eyes had a sort of darkened mask look and the top of his head looked almost as if there was a dark spot merging with his black hair. He appeared as if he could be some sort of extra dark East Indian with flat slender lips. "This is Singh. He is an engineer and works on the motors. Must power the tools, eh Singh?" Singh didn't even look up and simply responded with slight smile. "Must have. Don't want to be stuck without it." Mark looked around the office, papers and a wall board of printed and scribbled drawings where everywhere. Mark briefly noticed something about the Titu forest of Vular. The first names of locations he had seen. Generally it seemed, this guy either worked like a maniac or did not cleanup.

They quickly slipped out and continued meandering down the hallway. Jaul introduced him to a few more various people working on the project. Finally, Jaul led him down a hallway and into another large office area.

"Tink, one of your previous coworkers is here," Jaul announced. Looking around the corner, Tink located them. "Hey, Mark, whazzup?" Smirking slightly loftily, Mark responded, "What have you been up to over here, do? Unfortunately, we are on a different team project, yet at least, we are in the same building, eh?" "At least we can IM and e-mail each other within the company," Tink replied. "I'll be in our project room when you return so we can help you get started tomorrow," Jaul interjected. "Okay, thanks, Jaul," Mark said then turned back toward Tink. "How has it been here? What is it like working here? Did you notice anything odd about this place?" Tink lowered his tone quickly. "Thus far, the only thing odd about it is that most of the projects are on a need-to-know basis." Mark smiled nonchalantly and quietly said, "Keep your eyes peeled and let me know." Raising his voice a bit, he said, "Well, you have a great day. I'll talk to you later."

Returning to the main area, Jaul noticed his entry and immediately pointed him to his desk. "Here is your office, and while you do not have a window view yourself, the view is right across the hallway, immediately visible through the glass doors." Mark smiled, not sure that they even considered that. "Great! Thanks for thinking of me." Mark thought the solid dark-gray wall looked nicer than the other pastel yellow walls. The wall was surrounded by one glass wall with a door and two cubicle like partition walls. Mark arranged his desk and checked the content of his hard drive. Finally, Mark made for his car.

Chapter 9

Gone Missing

Mark opened the door, exiting to the parking lot while locating his Acura across the parking lot through the drenching downpour. Raindrops forcefully assaulted his exposed hands until Mark fitted his black leather gloves. Navigating his leather trench coat, Mark made his way to the driver's seat. Mark pulled out his tablet and quickly zapped a text before igniting the engine.

Reaching his house, Mark quickly sautéed some vegetables and steak tips while watching the current previews of upcoming movies. No response, odd, Mark said to himself. "There you are," a raspy voice said, causing Mark to jitter out of surprise, slightly spilling his espresso. The voice continued, "Your friend Ramses has some nice things. He should keep them better guarded. Not to worry, I'll be leaving. I had the displeasure of meeting your friendly spiders." Mark thought to himself, What the? My spiders? Ha, hopefully they beat the crap out of him. Mark then responded, "Ramses was probably not expecting thieves to visit while he was out. I am sure you would be the one surprised next time around."

There was no response to Marks retort. Mark intently scrutinized the room, especially where it seemed the voice's audio was coming from. However, it could have been on the other side of the crème colored wall and Mark could find nothing to indicate anything was unusual. However, he did find new satisfaction in the wall pattern which had a lightly painted green gradient grid pattern in a sort of curved three-dimensional fashion overlaying the crème wall. Mark returned and swiftly finished his espresso.

Quickly escaping to the garage, Mark zipped out into the heavy rain. Hugging the curves, Mark accelerated at a bit above the speed limit. The windshield wipers made a slight yet swift, sweeping and zipping noise with seemingly endless attempts to keep the window free of liquid rain. Turning to his tablet, he hit the redial only to again get Isis's machine. Mark could not help but wonder if Isis was well, and why she did not answer her phone.

Intently observing the road ahead, Mark suddenly had a sense of déjà vu. Mark slowed to carefully analyze a small dirt road that exited to the main road. There was something eerily familiar about it. Mark decided it would only take a minute and turned onto the small dirt road. A sense of revelation overcame Mark as he commented to himself, No! Really? Th--this is th-e road? The road appeared nearly identical to the one he frequently visited in his dreams. While he came from a different direction, it clearly either was its twin or it was, in fact, the road. For some reason, Mark had thought the road was simply a dreamscape invention and not an actual road he could locate. Finally, Mark decided he had better finish locating Isis, and he could explore the road later.

Arriving at her apartment, Mark quickly located her beautiful i8 Spider. Nothing appeared out of the ordinary about it. Mark knocked on the townhome door for a while; there was seemingly no response. Slipping around the back, Mark browsed the large glass doors. Mark thought it was slightly odd that in a distant large open field was a growling black almost sickly hyena with long scraggly straight hair with striped legs. The place was nearly empty, and only the largest of items were chaotically lying about. She did not say anything about moving, Mark thought while calling the police station.

Arriving on the scene was John Thomas again. "Hello, Mark. How well did you know Isis? I'll need a statement." Mark smirked. "Well enough. I think she would have told me if she was moving. I tried to call her all day. After there was no answer, I came out here to discover her townhouse in disarray. Do you need anything from me? Now that you are here, I figure on letting you do your job." John looked him up and down with thoughtfulness. "All I need to know is the last time she contacted you. Then we can investigate the scene, and you can go."

Slightly looking up yet not really "looking," Mark pondered that. "The . . . the last time . . . was two days ago. She called me on my tablet to see what was up and if I was going to have another party. I said not currently because of some strange thefts and that I would let her know." John quickly jotted some things down. "You tried to call her, and it was suspicious that she was not answering 'all day,' prompting you to drive out here and discover her townhouse apparently in disarray while her car was still here. Correct?" Mark said with a serious look, "Yes. I did not go inside. I merely observed from the windows." John closed his tablet computer cover to prevent the rain from touching the screen, "Great! Thank you, you may go."

While making his way back, Mark decided to stop at the road he had noticed on his way there. Turning off the main road, it was a small dirt road. After a short while it turned into a dusty trail, and he slowed then stopped. Looking around it was still light outside and he could view the landscape with ease. The short weedy grass blew lightly in the breeze. An exceptional view of the horizon reminded him he had a few hours left of daylight. Mark exited his vehicle and closed the door softly as if this was some sort of momentous occasion. Scanning the scene it looked sort of like his dream.

Mark began walking the dusty trail. After walking a short while, he could see a lone solitary tree with vibrant green leaves. Mark muttered to himself while intently scrutinizing every detail of what his visual cortex was displaying to his mind. "Is…that the tree?! It must be. It looks like it." A small breeze delivered a wisp of dust and grass in the otherwise clean smelling air. It was almost as if something was responding to his discovery. Mark carefully examined his slightly shaking hand and realized he was unsure of what might be here that he cannot see while in a waking state.

Mark turned and examined the travel path that he had been walking. The grass appeared to whisk in a circular manner with the breeze as if somehow pointing to his trail. An old shoe was resting a few inches away from where he had walked. The old shoe suddenly gave him a strong feeling of déjà vu, as if it was somehow an old friend. Mark mumbled as he retraced his steps. "Thank you old friend." Mark decided it was time to return home and exited to his car.

Walking around the car, John carefully analyzed every detail. The finger print duster was still delicately at work on the inside. Looking back John could still see Tina's dead corpse, in route to the coroners, almost in the ambulance. The flashing turn signal light was annoying especially in combination with the windshield wiper. "Turn those things off as soon as you can, please." The finger print duster who was putting everything away quickly reached over and shut the car off.

Softly approaching Thoth announced, "So what do we have thus far." John zapped back, "Nothing. No finger prints except the victim. It's like the car suddenly just drove off the road." Thoth responded in a matter of fact tone, "The body has been here for a while; several hours at least. No houses nearby and anyone driving by would have thought it was nothing." John showed a bit of surprise, "Really, and the car was on the whole time? I wonder if there was someone else that drove her here."

John carefully examined the car seats. "Well, no evidence to prove another person was in the car. However, we cannot rule it out. " Thoth interjected, "Well, another mysterious event. Did you check for more of that aluminum oxide material?" John turned towards Thoth, "Why yes, there does appear to be a small amount of it over here near the wheel. They may utilize it to coat something." John pointed to the steering wheel.

Waltzing into the new office, Mark had the taste of his morning espresso lingering on his tongue. He sat at his desk, started his computer and began perusing the document that had been purposely placed on his keyboard. Looking up, Mark noticed Jaul slip in and meander a short way from the door. "Morning, Mark, I am going to help you get started on our new project. Understand, we are working on the next-generation product, and the current version is selling well from what I hear," Jaul cheerfully elaborated while nursing a cup of coffee. Jaul was dressed pretty much the same as yesterday, only the shirt had a slightly different yet similar pattern. Jaul's hair hung past his ears yet short enough as to not reach his shoulders, and it was a bit more frazzled today with no real shine. Mark gleamed back. "Morning, and here I was, going to try to dive in and understand it myself. Awesome."

The two of them turned suddenly to acknowledge the arrival of Dek. "I am singing in the rain today!" A beaming Jaul, responded with nearly his entire body. "What is up?" Dek looked at Mark and then at Jaul with enthusiasm and said, "Moments ago, I was in a board meeting. Sales of our explorer class are up 20 percent from last month, and it sounds like we are going to have some new clients! I presented it to Darkwaters, the underwater resource miners, and it was like selling itself. It felt like I was practically stealing the deal. The potential for so much profit was there." Mark smiled with a bit of a chuckle. "Great! So you will want the next generation vehicle that we are working on which will allow you to make some more stealing deals." Dek smiled in confirmation. "Absolutely, glad to have you on the team."

Jaul was still looking at Dek. "I was showing Mark the part he will be working on so he could get started." Dek smiled and responded, "Of course, of course. I had to tell you guys how things are going. Sounds like we are going places today! Talk at you guys later!" With that, Dek strolled out of the office. Jaul turned to Mark. "Great news, eh? How about you look over the Stinger project's system files and get to know it for now. Let me know if you have any questions at all." Jaul turned quickly and made for his own office.

Mark opened one of the project's PDF files and began coming to grips with the product when his instant messenger started flashing. It was Tink asking him how it was going, and Mark responded in kind. Tink then messaged, "Did hear from Dek about product sales? Great, eh? Good for business, good for our contracts."

Mark responded, "Yeah, that is good for now anyway. Did you look around? Did you notice anything unusual?" Tink responded with a frown, "Do, no. Nothing unusual. Only the usual company business to make the product and sell it. I, for one, am glad they are going to make some money so I can keep my contract and possibly get an extension when it is up."

Ah, Tink is going with the pocketbook. Mark did not blame him for that. Mark then responded, "Okay, well, several people have had things stolen. I cannot talk about it now." Tink responded, "You and your conspiracy theory. Who really cares if there are blind people working here? Wake up and smell the coffee, bud." With that, Tink placed his instant messenger in do not disturb mode.

Mark reviewed the schematics, plans, and objectives for several hours before zipping up his jacket. Wondering what Tink was up to Mark zapps him an instant message. "Tink my friend. Why are you here so late?" Tink zapps back with sunglass smiley. "OT pays the bills with a little extra." Mark smiles at his hard working friend's candor. "What about we make the leap to the Cyberpad?"

Tink's response took a few moments. "I would like to, however, I must linger with blood." Mark chuckles at Tinks wording. "Did you use a time machine recently? Blood really? In the modern era we utilize DNA to determine TRUE relatives. The gene is far more accurate and correct than the old archaic term 'blood'." Tink quickly zapped back an 'lol' and a laughing smiley. Mark continued while chuckling to himself loftily, "Really. The term 'blood' was used when people did not know much about the subject. Parents often don't even have the same blood type! Well anyway, have fun with the relatives."

Mark decided that it might be nice to meet with some of his new affiliates and swiftly began instant messaging Larkul to gauge his current state. "How are you this fine evening?" Larkul replied back after a slight delay. "Doing well. It has been busy, yet seems to be coming together." Pondering his next query, Mark quickly responded. "What are your plans after work? Perhaps we could review project notes and socialize a bit." Larkul responded with frown smiley. "I must crash man; I have been working long hard hours." Mark smirked at that. "That is why you optimize you sleeping patterns. So you sleep less and live more without the crash later. Really, it is much better." Larkul responded quickly. "Yea, well I push it a bit at times. Have a nice evening. Perhaps later, I'll take you up on that."

It was a wet one outside, and Mark made a run for the car. Brushing off the wet, Mark made himself comfortable in his Acura when, suddenly, his tablet announced that someone was calling. Answering, Mark was a bit surprised that the police had video on the phone, yet there he was, Officer John. "I was calling to let you know that Isis is now a missing person. We won't officially announce it for at least five days from the incident in case she is not a missing person at all. That is the shortest timeframe I can do, you understand? Since her car is still at her apartment and there were signs of odd, possibly chaotic, activity inside, the evidence suggests she was possibly abducted, which is how we came up with the five-day timetable. I did some preliminary research on her whereabouts and came up empty." Mark frowned. "Not good. Thanks for letting me know." John continued, "If you come upon any information concerning her whereabouts, make sure you let us know ASAP." Mark was concerned yet glad to be in the loop. "Will do, thank you." Where are you, Isis? Mark thought to himself as he raced for his dry garage.

Walking through the doorway, Mark noticed his tablet notifying him of a text. The text read, "Whazzup? Can I come over? I need to come over." It was Mairis, and Mark texted back, "Sure thing, see you in a bit." Very shortly, another text showed. "Sifive, Mark. I am here at Ramses' place, helping him secure his place after the burglary. Did you want to hang out at Ramses' place?" This time, it was Garrick with the sifive hello, which was their version of a high-five hello. Mark texted back, "Well, Mairis is coming over, so perhaps another time. So Isis and Tina are now missing persons, according to Officer John. However, he cannot pursue it too much until after five days have passed so as to make it official." Garrick responded with a frown. "Bum deal, I'll keep an eye out."

Garrick continued, "I visited Dacian's house to see if I could see or hear anything obvious about it, and I came up with nothing. There seems to be nothing really unusual about it or the area. I did discover that Chris Vocal is also blind and the owner of the company. On the other hand, I had an encounter with one of our vocal friends." Mark texted back, "Really, what happened? I mean what did the so-called voice say?"

Garrick responded, "Well, it told me to keep to my own business and would not comment about any thefts. The thing slightly threatened me if I get a little too nosy. I assume that either I picked up on it at Ramses' place, the Cyberpad, Dacian's, or somewhere in between." Mark made a smirking smiley. "Well, that narrows it down. It could have been any of those places. If it had something to do with Ramses' robbery, it may have been there. On the other hand, it could be saying that because you were checking out Dacian's place. Also, I noticed some unusual references to places I've never seen before while I was at work today. See what you can find about 'Vular' and the Titu Forest." Garrick responded, "Will do. I also plan on paying a visit to Chris Vocal's abode. I'll let you know how it goes."

Staring at the object, Mairis commented, "This is a really interesting piece. Where did you get this?" Mark was walking with two fresh hot espressos in hand and said, "It is collateral for loan. If or when Josh can pay me what is owed, then I'll return the captive art to him." Mark could not help to think that Mairis is looking more like Tia all the time, perhaps even a little better than in his dreams. Mairis carefully examined the protruding jungle tree elements of the three-dimensional object. It was primarily a painted object that appeared as a sort of three-dimensional passageway to a wild jungle region. The painted imagery also had three dimensions, giving the illusion of an actual passageway. The painted picture was a bit rough, which was probably done on purpose, yet seemed eerily real as if there actually was a way to step through it into the wild jungle.

"So, sad about Tina." Mairis softly held Marks hand. "That was incredibly unfortunate; she was so much fun too. There was so much potential for a fun friendship." Mairis looked into Marks eyes longingly. Mark responded in kind and continued, "I would go after her if I didn't know she was currently located in the morgue. I'll look into the possibility of her essence being still around. Hopefully, she is birthed into a better hereafter." Mairis acknowledged the situation with a limited smile and slightly turned her head to lean on Mark.

Looking around, Tina was lying in a large slightly comfortable bed. Where am I, she thought to herself. Reaching to free herself from the down comforter, she immediately noticed her hands were different. It was much younger than she was expecting. Quickly locating a mirror she peered into the mirror with awe. Had she somehow found a time machine or grown younger? She looked like she did when she was in her early teenage years. She was still like herself, only ten years younger. "Woa!", she announced out loud.

Looking around the quaint room, it was full of frills and pastels. Dainty little decors mixed with modern older things. The room was like something she might have had at such an age, yet never remembered living in. Suddenly, from a dark corner a raspy voice said, "Welcome to your new home Tina, or shall we call you Jara?" Carefully, Tina made for the door and slowly opened it. "Jara, honey breakfast is ready." Announced an elder female voice, possibly her mother? Tina thought to herself again, Where the heck am I?

Chapter 10

Dueling Forces

Reaching for the door, Mark thought to himself, at least it wasn't raining today. The overcast sky loomed, yet the cumuli were not quite as dark as yesterday, providing a glimmer of blue sky. Mark quickly located his desk and was loading the CAD software when his messenger started notifying him. It was Tink. "Hey, can I visit? It's my break, and I tire of sitting at my desk." Tink had an earlier shift that he selected by choice. Mark quickly zapped back. "Sure, you know where my desk is, correct?" Turning his head, Mark noticed Jaul at his door. "Whats up, Jaul?" Jaul smiled. "How are you doing familiarizing yourself with everything?" Mark responded, "So far so good, it's Tink's break. Is it okay if he visits for a bit?" Jaul zapped back. "Sure, no problems. This is a comfortable environment, if you haven't noticed. As long as you are getting work done."

Mark smirked, pleased with the response. "So how is biz? Everything okay on the improving sales front?" Jaul looked slightly to the side, his eyes shifted, and he slightly frowned. "Well actually, those sales are costing us more money than anticipated. Sales are up, yet so are costs. So it is a bit up in the air right now, how it will go." Mark, tapping his pen, showed a serious look. "Okay, let me know if there is something I can do. I'll be working on the new sensor tech as requested for now." Jaul smiled widely, and his body movement went with the smile. "Sure, thank you, and I'll let you know."

Tink slipped past Jaul in the doorway, with a minor acknowledgment of each other. Mark, observing the encounter, smiled at Tink. "Whazzup! Tink!" Tink smiled, handing Mark a clear plastic bottle. "Would you like bottled water?" Mark nodded his head. "Sure, thanks." Tink made himself comfortable on the edge of the desk and looked at Mark. His long dark hair was slightly shorter now. "So how do you like this versus designing video games?" Mark, fixing his wavy yet short auburn hair, as a sort of auto-reflex, responded, "I'm not sure yet. Designing video games was quite fun, yet this tool will be utilized to explore and detect things, so that will also be interesting. The video game design is a bit more creative."

Tink smiled quickly, sipped his water, and then moved his hair out of his face. He touched his head briefly and continued, "Why do you make those things up in your video games? I mean, in the last video game you designed, a city called Olympia of the Pacific Northwest rather than the real city of Olympus on Lake Victoria. There were some things that were a little similar, yet it was nearly always rainy and it seemed to have too many evergreen trees around, in my opinion. Why lie like that? Why not simply call it Olympus? More like the real thing we live with?" Mark laughed, shaking his entire chair slightly. "Well, it needed to be like the player is reaching into another dimension yet feel sort like they've been somewhere similar, at least for that game."

Tink continued, "What about the people who don't live in Olympus? I suppose they can look it up, yet if they look up Olympia, they may not find Olympus. What was with Memphis on the great Misipi River with gumbo trees? Why not simply palms in the paradigm of the Nile, like the real Memphra? Why make up such fictional places [like Olympia and Memphis]?" Mark still smirked. "Well, it is a real place, like another thread to the multiverse, another dimension. They step into the video game and explore. It is not meant to be an exact replica of the cities we know as Olympus or Memphra, although I possibly should have placed some palm trees in Memphis."

"Do, you must know, you've played the game. Didn't you like exploring the game universe that I designed? Why so skeptical?" Tink started laughing and looked him in the eye after chugging on his water. "I'm just messing with you, do. I know it's another world for the gamer to explore. Have you ever thought from a different perspective like that? Like, you created something that wasn't real?" Mark, relieved, relaxed his arms on his chair. "Ha! Very funny. No, not really. To me, they are real places, real threads in another dimension. Most real things have a design phase. It's a tough job, yet someone's got to do it."

What a conversation. Was he simply trying to have fun, or were there subtle hints, trying to suggest what I did before wasn't real? Good luck with that one. Mark continued, "Don't let this place get to you, do." Tink laughed it off. "Well, I had an epiphany the other day and was thinking about our previous work. I had to discuss it with someone. I better get back to work. Talk later, do."

Mark continued analyzing the schematics of the underwater sea vehicle; it only slightly varied from the space version of the vehicle. The objective was to ensure the maximum effectiveness of the sensors and capabilities in as many situations as possible. Initial sensor was obvious; make room and place one inside the vehicle's drill. This way, it could take measurements of the area of the drill target. Often, the objective was to see, hear, touch, or otherwise detect things that were difficult to see. He spent the rest of the day examining various possible positions.

Approaching his house, Mark noticed a solitary white lark with black wings standing in the center of his walkway. Parking his car in his garage, Mark slipped in the garage doorway to his house.

Swiftly grabbing a scoop of coffee, Mark started a cup of espresso. Mark's tablet suddenly notified him of a call, and he quickly grabbed it. "Mark here." He knew it wasn't Garrick because they had a silence code to avoid detection. A picture of Josh came into view. "Hey, Mark. What's up!" Mark smiled while wiping his hands. "Josh, how are you on this fine day?" Mark reached over and turned on his computerized TV system. Josh then continued, "Guess what? I have your three hundred thousand credits." Mark, now excited yet also a little disappointed, said, "Awesome. I did really like your art and will regret seeing it go. However, the 300K will come in handy. When do you want to arrange for the exchange?" Josh chuckled. "Can I pick it up today?" Mark responded, "Sure, as long as I can verify funds. I'll be here the rest of the day. Feel free to deposit the funds into my PayPal account."

"I'll make the transfer now. I'm on my way." Josh stated with a smile and swiftly ended the call. A mere 10 minutes passed with Mark comfortably sipping his espresso and watching the news before Marks door alarm announced. Mark grabbing his tablet casually made his way toward the door while his senses tingled with satisfaction seemingly in the thick atmosphere of his home.

Reaching the door, Mark recognized Josh. "So, you finally mustered the credits, eh?" Josh made a broad smile while fidgeting with his shirt. "Yes. Yes. Did you confirm the funds?" Mark smiled with confidence as he smoothly waved his arm indicating that Josh come in. "Not yet, let me do that." Quickly tapping his tablet a few times, Mark pulled up the transaction and it showed completed with a confirmation number.

Immediately behind Josh were two work men dressed all in white holding a container. The men walked towards the large three dimensional art piece and began preparing the container for transport. Josh looked at Mark. "It is in excellent condition, and looks even better than the day I let you hold it." Mark smiled while confidently standing in a slightly relaxed manner. "I had it touched up. Well, it was in the middle of my main foyer." Josh laughed as he exited immediately behind the movers. "Alright, thanks again."

After a long day, Mark was glad to have an extra three hundred thousand credits and made his way to his large comfortable bed. Soon, Mark shifted into sleep, finding himself in the field he had frequently visited.

Mark was walking along the dirt road; on the side were two bright blue frogs with slightly hunched backs. He thought to himself that he should put some feelers out to find Tina. A short distance away, there appeared to be several people running to and fro around a luminous cloud of sorts. They were utilizing what appeared to be nets and mirrors.

A sticky large thick black liquid began flowing out of the cloud. In the distance, there was a large dam holding back an unknown amount of water. A small leak in the dam was allowing water to turn what was a dry riverbed into a small stream. Fortunately, the dam showed no signs of breaking further for now.

Mark looked again at the cloud and thought; I hope this doesn't have anything to do with Tina. Immediately, the men grabbed several mirrored large flat shovels and began shoveling the liquid back into the cloud as much as possible. A large black figure rose out of the liquid; even the eyes were black. Leaping towards the figure, Mark focused his eyes which emanated thick hot forceful waves. The black figure responded in kind after withstanding several blows from the waves and attempted to force Mark toward the ground. Mark leaped backward and then attempted to repeat the performance. The black figure suddenly returned to liquid then swiftly oozed in a sort of zigzagged pattern toward Mark.

"Mark, don't worry. I like it better here, I wish you well, but I've moved on." It was Tina, she is still alive! Well, sort of, somewhere in space and time. Suddenly, one of the men said, "Close the portal, they're coming through the portal! It is either that, or we'll have to kill them." It was unusual for speech to be in the dream, and that was the only thing said throughout the dream. Mark opened his eyes with force to the usual patterns on the ceiling.

Garrick cautiously approached the lining of buses and trees that surrounded an open plane. A small dirt road led to a large neatly enclosed rock covered space obviously utilized for parking. A short distance away was an unusually tall and elaborate building with a pastel blue exterior. The building appeared to be possibly five stories high, six if one counted the attic area. Not only was it tall, it appeared to spread for quite a distance.

"This place is massive", Garrick mumbled to himself. Crawling through the bushes, he could see lights coming from inside. "Blind man that needs lights? He must have visitors, caretakers or something." He slowly made his way across the open space in the most unobvious way he could.

The vibes coming from the environment were very unusual. Garrick's extremely perceptive senses were still trying understand what it was he was picking up on. It felt as though something was out of place either him or the building. Not only that, but space seemed stretched almost distorted. "Very odd", he muttered to himself.

Reaching the side wall of the large mansion, Garrick noticed an unusually dark black corner. He approached the corner which now appeared to be nearly unnaturally "black". Garrick then scanned the area; nobody seemed to be within viewing range.

Reaching into his satchel, Garrick located a small gun like "tool". Steadily he aimed at the corner and pressed a button on his interface. A spread of high charged ionic particles illuminated every crevice of the corner. "This light 'gun' is awesome", he thought to himself.

Surprisingly, the black briefly withstood and continued to cover the space. Slowly the dark covering burst into little "lit" particles before dissipating. "Well, it did not speak, say anything or even make a noise at all so it must not have been one our odd intruders. Could it be some sort of camouflage material?"

Garrick decided to make a swift exit due to a large increase in noise coming from inside the house. Intent was to avoid being "found out" in the event someone could somehow detect what he had momentarily done. Despite the unusual vibes, his senses didn't really prove anything. The freshly discovered black material most certainly was a good 'possible' connection to the intruders, yet Garrick decided it did not convict Vocal of anything. They could be spying on Chris much like they were Mark.\

The smell of the forest was well known to forest ranger Anthony Rossi. The air breezed swiftly by his nostrils fresh and crisp. Reaching with his right hand he single handedly grasped the Meconi's sub sandwich he was enjoying. The sky and atmosphere was warm and sunny which most of the wild life seemed to notice as well. Setting his sandwich down on his pickup, he marked the location on his tablet to notate that he had checked for contaminate levels. It was clean and beautiful as usual.

An odd shift in the wind caused Anthony to look up. "That was cold, how strange", he said to himself. Grabbing his binoculars, he scanned the area. Off in the distance the sky was nearly black with something.

He monitored it for a moment and realized it was a pack of Falcons. "How *extremely* unusual. That is not normal for Falcons to do that. I'm going to have to check it out." Talking to 'himself' out in the wilderness was not unusual. Whom else would he talk to?

The off-road pickup breezed quickly towards the vicinity. As he approached, Tony slowed to maintain a bit more stealth since this could be something criminal. Easier to hide out here, he thought to himself.

Tony slowed to a crawl then he grabbed his binoculars to take a closer look at what he was seeing. He noticed a large white truck marked as Zurich Movers, Inc. Several men were apparently loading the vehicle with quite a large quantity of what appeared to be used stuff. "I had better call it in to be safe", he said to himself.

Officer John Thomas had the helicopter land far enough away as to not draw suspicion and was immediately escorted in a black low-emission SUV. "What do you have for me?" He queried the local officer in charge. "With all the thefts going around we thought we had better check it out, and it does appear slightly suspicious. We did notice some of the aluminum oxide on the road to this location. However, any electronic equipment such as tablets must be turned off because we cannot detect any signals. We do require probable cause to proceed."

John quickly tapped his tablet a few times after a few moments he announced, "I have located a signal." The officer's jaw dropped, "How did you do that? We have been scanning for hours." John casually explained, "Some tablets have an anti-theft device. When the tablet is turned off they give off a really weak short range signal on a specific frequency. The signals are powered by an internal battery and are intended to last a very long time. The purpose is for times like this, so the tablet can be located."

John smirked then continued, "Let's see if we can ID this one. Nice! It is one of the missing persons, Isis and her brother's tablet is there as well. No guarantee anyone is alive, however." John quickly looked around and then back to Thoth, "Get ready to move." They spread out as much as possible and covered the only road in and out. Finally announcing over a loud speaker, "Place your hands where we can see them. You are all under arrest!"

Sett was caught off guard entirely by the announcement, and immediately ducked behind the truck. He yelled, "Come and take me!" Most of his men had apparently pulled their weapons and began firing on what they could see of the police. The police began firing in response and John announced, "We have you surrounded. Put down your weapons, and come out with your hands were we can see them."

After a brief fire fight, most of Sett's men were surrendering while others made a run for it. John and the police advanced on their position and began arresting the perpetrators. John cautiously maneuvered around the truck with his weapon drawn when suddenly a bullet shredded through his right hand causing him to drop his weapon. Looking around the corner it was Sett himself and he was apparently an excellent shot. Sett fired again hitting John in the leg and said, "They gave me their electronics." John wincing in pain responded, "Then why fight if you will be exonerated?" Several officers tried to find a good place to position themselves.

Several clicking noised came from Sett's gun; He was out of ammo. Quickly he tried to reach for more. Enduring the pain, John jolted toward Sett and grabbed onto his arm. Sett reached around slammed on John's lower thigh where the bullet wound was. John stammered, yet endured and tried to slam him against the truck with all his body weight. Sett twisted under the pressure making a small plea at the pain of his twisted leg at the same time landing John on the ground. John reached out and grabbed Sett's twisted leg then pulled causing Sett to fall to the ground. Sett immediately reached for the ammunition, but was too late. Several officers surrounded him with weapons drawn. Thoth zapped confidently, "Go for it bud. Give us the satisfaction of gunning you down."

Sipping on his espresso, Mark reach for his tablet. Mark texted Garrick a quick zap. "These intruders that we are dealing with may actually be migrating from somewhere. It makes sense that they are not locals. Possibly even somewhere far away. I could not find anything on Vular or Titu forest. With the exception to a fictitious reference to an old myth, there was not a whim. Perhaps places in a video game or book might have a reference to the myth?" Mark noticed a quick reply from Garrick. "I thought as much, I've never noticed these ..uh.. things around here before. It seems odd for them to have places in a video game around his office, especially that office." Mark finished his coffee before exiting for the office.

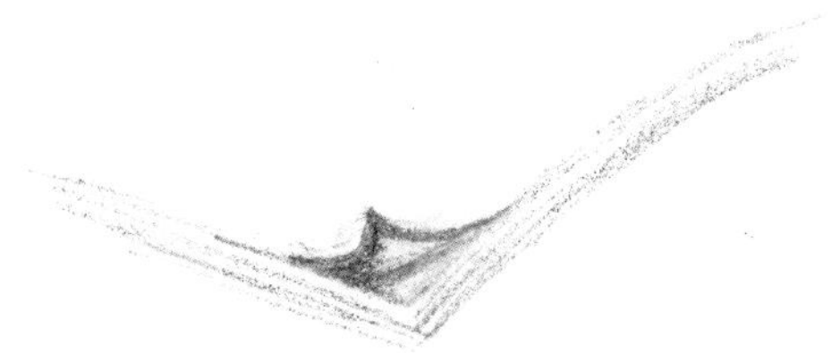

He clicked his remote. Mark's Acura announced that his alarm was monitoring as he reached for the door to the office. Mark had spent that last few days positioning various sorts of sensors in optimal positions and was nearly ready for a prototype sensor. The drill alone would detect material compositions, density of the surrounding soil, and even try to see up to one hundred meters.

Mark returned to his desk when Dek approached. Mark turned, facing Dek. "Hello, Mark, how are you?" Mark smirked. "Doing well. I am about to request a prototype, actually." With a serious look and slightly shifty eyes, Dek continued, "Well, that is great. You keep working on the next system. Unfortunately, we may not be able to ship the next model since some investors pulled out, and sales are costing more. We are no longer running profits. Currently, I am full-time tasked with locating new profits and/or investors." Mark turned serious. "Well, that is unfortunate. I will continue to do my job until told otherwise." Mark then smirked and continued, "Or you fail to pay my paychecks . . ." Dek smiled nonchalantly. "Okay, no problem. I'll let you know if there are any changes to your position."

Mark seated himself and sipped on his coffee before submitting his CAD file to the prototype printer. It would take a few days for it to be completely functional. From there, he tinkered with some optional configurations after breaking for lunch. Finally, he checked the Web for some new sensor technology before logging off for the day.

Grabbing his keys, Mark made for his Acura TLX. The sky was clear and blue; the sun was hidden by the nearby buildings yet was obviously colorful. The air was clean, slightly warm, and breezy. Reaching his car, he opened his door. Mark shuddered as, suddenly, that same hissing sound he had heard way back when this began was detected to his right. He immediately looked in its direction; he could see nothing there. Suddenly, the raspy voice said, "You will not stop us. We are coming in as we please." Mark jumped at the sound of the voice. "Now, now. We will deal with you. It is better for you if you stay on your side of the fence. Tell me where Tina is." It laughed and hissed a bit. Mark simply exited the parking lot in his Acura.

Chapter 11

The Returning

Mark was preparing his regular espresso when his tablet notified him of a text. Mark swiftly examined it; it was Isis! Isis texted him, “Sorry, I missed your calls. I was with my brother. It is a long story.” Mark responded, “Oh my! Do you want to meet at the Cyberpad and tell me all about it?” Isis texted back, “Not tonight. I want to, though. How about tomorrow after I rest up?”

The next day after work, Mark sat in the low chair and reached for his energy drink on the glass table. The atmosphere was filled with some computerized dubstep with a hyper fast beat. The sliding doors opened, and Mark looked up; it was Isis. She waltzed in; her shimmering black hair bounced yet seemed to stick together in near unison. Her bright-green leather jacket tightly gripped her upper body and matched quite nicely with her darker yet still-green skirt, which tightly bounced around her knees. She slipped off her black leather gloves then unzipped and removed her jacket leisurely, revealing a black with shimmering-green zigzag-pattern rayon top. The rayon top had a darkened brass zipper that was slightly unzipped, revealing her upper chest. Isis smiled almost seductively as she walked.

“Hi, Mark. Whazzup!” Isis said as she sat down on the nearby chair in a very comfortable sprawling leisurely manner. “Isis! You’re here! I have been very worried about you for quite some time. I called you frequently, and when you did not answer, eventually, I drove to your place. Your spider was still on-site, yet your apartment was in disarray with a lot of things removed. At which point, I called the police,” Mark elaborated, partially utilizing hand gestures. Isis sighed with a slight smile. “Yeah, thank you so much for your concern. At least someone cared about my welfare!" "No problem. Now it's your turn. What happened?" Mark smirked loftily.

Isis enthusiastically sat up. "Yes. First, I will order." Isis looked toward the counter. Mark, smirking, touched his tablet and placed the order. Isis looked at him. "Thank you." The drink was delivered to their table almost as quickly as they placed the request. Isis grabbed her large twenty-four-ounce can and chugged a bit more than a sip. "Ahh."

She turned toward Mark and continued, "Okay, so I woke up that Friday morning and began the usual Friday morning thing when my brother Geb showed at my door. I was really happy to see my brother. However, he had a new friend with him. First, I did not think much of it as Geb introduced me to Sett. Oddly, Geb was aware that I had Friday off that week and he wanted to go to a cabin in a secluded area on Mount Zurich."

Shifting her hair away from her face and sipping her energy drink, Isis continued, "Anyway, so I resisted at first, and then Geb pulled me aside and pleaded with me. He did not want to go alone with Sett and thought it would be 'so much more fun.' I wasn't even suspicious of Sett. I m-mean, he was supposedly a friend of Geb, who I trusted. Eventually, I said I would go only after we chased each other around the house for a while." Mark laughed. "You have an interesting relationship with your brother." Isis smirked. "Yeah, well, we grew up together, you know." Her face shifted intensity as she continued, "As I was saying, the stuff in my house got moved around a bit. Then Geb insisted that I take more than simply weekend garb and started packing my things in the truck outside. After a brief scuffle with him, I notice something different about him. It was like he wasn't himself or something."

Relaxing herself in the chair, she continued, "Little did we realize that Sett also removed items from my house after we left. We traveled for hours after picking up some traveling supplies. The road eventually turned to a dirt road, which we continued to travel for quite some time before locating the cabin. The cabin seemed quite nice, actually with a lot of bedrooms, and at first, I was thinking it was actually going to turn out to be fun, like bro had insisted. We enjoyed ourselves all day long, yet while we were doing as such"—sipping her beverage, her face showed a more serious look as she continued—"Sett insisted that this trip be a technology 'detox' event and convinced Geb to turn over all our technology, including our phones. My domain that I designed and assembled, I was to wean myself from. Of all the balls! Meanwhile, Sett's friends were relocating our stuff where they intended on selling it off.

Mark scoffed loftily shifting his eyes as if he had been complimented. "'Detox'? While technology is a material it's not quite the same as substance abuse. For one, it can still be around years after use. I do understand the addictive qualities of it I—suppose yet it is not quite a substance." Mark smirking looked back at Isis. "Please, continue."

"The next morning, I awoke, and the door to our room was sealed shut. There was no exit. Since it was obviously preplanned, Sett must have made sure there were no obvious exits besides the door." Isis rolled her eyes. "I could have killed Geb. We turned all our computer equipment to Sett, including my tablet. We screamed at the door for what must have been hours and hours. We did not even have a clock to know what time it was. The only window was a strong Plexiglas, and we could not easily break it. Geb continued to hope that Sett would come forth and open the door, so he constantly yelled at the door, asking Sett to be reasonable. Of course, I started to get furious with both of them."

Isis, sipping her beverage, shifted in her seat and briefly fixed her hair then continued with a sort of fascination on her face. "Eventually, I calmed down because it wasn't helping, when I noticed outside the window a peregrine falcon look in the window with an unusual curiosity. I could tell it was a peregrine by the marking around its eye. I tried yelling at it to get help. I even tried sign language. Out of frustration, I focused and charged the window, slamming against it with unusual strength. It actually cracked and broke revealing a second window an inch away. The police tell me that should never have happened. Even bullets could not crack that particular window. The falcon showed no fear even after I did that and only looked more curious than ever. I screamed at it, 'Get help, bitch!' I thought, perhaps, it was a pet and looked for signs of such. There were none. No tags, harness marks, or anything. It suddenly flew away, and at the same time, an enormous amount of birds in the trees also flew. The sky nearly turned black with birds. I just thought that was so weird. A short while later, the falcon returned to the window!"

Isis began smirking vividly. "Apparently, a ranger had noticed the bird's odd behavior and decided to investigate. The ranger then observed Sett and crew loading our stuff when he decided to contact the police. The police detected it as unusual, and the stuff being loaded was also unusual. Anyway, they somehow picked up my tablet signal from inside the truck and found that I was reported missing. Finally, Officer John came to the rescue and raided the place. I was still attempting to communicate with the falcon that had been outside the window the entire time when the raid occurred. Moments after the raid started, the falcon—which must have been there for hours—suddenly flew away and did not return. The police recovered all of our stuff, and

Geb suddenly seemed his usual self again." Isis sighed and relaxed as she ended the story. "I am so glad to be back to designing and assembling my domain in this world!"

Mark looked a bit into the air at seemingly nothing, "Wow! What a story. Did you ever fear the worst?" Isis smiled as she responded, "Not really, it did not seem like my life was threatened at the time, although I suppose Sett could have walked in with a gun at any time, especially since we were making such intense announcements." Mark chugged his energy drink and said, "Did you think perhaps the falcon was there with intent on keeping you company while the police figured it out?" Isis chuckled with her whole body. "Well, it did seem like a wild bird, so I wasn't sure what its intent was. It was very odd how unfrightened it was of us and how it lead to our discovery." They both looked up at the giant falcon in the Cyberpad and simultaneously said "Thank you." After which, they both erupted into laughter.

After a late night with Isis at the Cyberpad, Mark returned home and located his large comfortable bed. Quickly shifting to another state of mind, he found himself in a field of the usual dusty road. The grassy field extended toward the horizon while behind him was the beginning of a forest, and there was a slight breeze coming in the direction of the dimly lit horizon. A short while away, the luminous cloud was much smaller yet still there. Suddenly, several smaller black gas-like clouds descended upon the field from an unknown location.

Mark quickly generated a sphere of energy then squeezed it that generated waves of thick energy, assaulting the small "ghosts." The dark "ghosts" suddenly began emitting an extremely high-pitched noise that Mark could barely hear. Off in the distance, glass began cracking and breaking from the noise, presumably the nearby houses. It barely affected Mark who was thinking, wrong move. Slamming the ground, large energy waves echoed toward the "ghosts." The waves reached the "ghosts" and shredded them in a misty substance that landed on the ground lifelessly. Mark jolted out of surprise when the misty substance reconstituted momentarily back into small clouds as before. Only this time several of them had white noses. Their noses previously were not discernible since they appeared to simply be black clouds of mist in the air. However, they quickly retreated into the distance.

Mark reached into his pocket and pulled out an eagle's feather, a symbol of an eye, and a small brightly illuminated sphere, representing various things. He placed them on the ground on top of one another. Placing his hands facing each other just above the items on the ground, he spread them away and near each other repeatedly back and forth evenly until his hands felt each other even without touching. Suddenly, everything flashed bright-yellowish white then began to come into focus.

It was similar to the setting in one of his video game scenes. "Hello?" a female voice said with a very inquisitive tone. "Who is there?" It was dark outside, and he could see only parts of the tree line. Mark turned to face the voice. "I-I'm Mark Khiop." "Oh, I know you. The . . . the multithread guy. I have been reading about you. With the spiders?" Mark smiled. "Really, you've been reading about me? What did it say?" Without warning, everything flashed bright-yellowish white again, and Mark was standing near the items he had set on the ground.

"It worked! Of all the places and threads I have been!" Mark exclaimed. "Now if only I can make it work for a bit longer, I'll have completed my objective." Mark continued thinking as he picked up his symbols. Placing them in his pocket, Mark could not help but notice that the portal where the black ooze had come from was gone. Awesome. I had no interest in visiting them. Hopefully, it is closed, he thought to himself. Mark awoke and looked at the window, the morning light blasting through.

Reaching his tablet, Mark quickly texted Garrick, "I had an encounter with some black ghosts in the dreamscape." After like ten minutes while Mark relaxed in bed before starting the day, Garrick responded with a text. "Really, what happened?" Mark exuberantly responded, "Well, they are now plagued at least I think their noses are. It happened during normal combat and they retreated." Garrick delayed response, "Wow! Lol" Mark added, "It wasn't really on purpose, it was a fight. Unless, of course, it was coincidental which seems unlikely."

Chapter 12

Closure and Revelation

Mark relocated his leather trench coat, allowing him to exit his vehicle smoothly. Mark slipped into the building and made for the coffee machine. Today, he should have his prototype for testing, and he figured a new product might be helpful to Dek. Even though he did not care that much, these people were with people who were stealing from him and his friends. Mark was professional, yet most importantly, it was better to learn 'what he could' from the inside than to quit. Large coffee in hand, Mark waltzed down the hallway to the manufacturing lab. Swiping his badge, Mark opened the door then swiftly found his way to the work-order desk. Again, he swiped his badge and tapped the screen where the selection for his project was. Turning quickly, Mark sat down on the simple yet elegant chairs lined up along the wall for waiting.

An engineer in a large white cloak approached the desk then looked directly at him. "Mark, I presume." Mark smiled casually. "Yes, that's me." Glancing at the screen and then again at Mark, he said, "Unfortunately, all prototype production has been put on standby. For now, you will have to wait. Please, discuss this with your project manager. Have a good day!" With that, the engineer swiftly exited the room without even looking at Mark.

Mark was a little taken aback by that. What the? Mark swiftly returned to his desk and loaded up his computer. "Nothing unusual here," Mark mumbled to himself. He checked his calendar; all still normal and no cancellations on it. Finishing his coffee, Mark slipped down the hallway and knocked on Dek's door. "Come in, come in." Dek gestured. "I have been advised there will be no prototype productions. Is there something I need to know?" Mark queried, a bit unsure.

Dek showed perspiration on his forehead as he wiped his nose. Dek responded with a sigh, "Unfortunately, the project is suspended for now. I was going to inform you tomorrow, yet I understand you have discovered it before I could. Right now, this company is in for a rough ride and may not make it. All future projects are suspended until further notice." Mark turned serious, "Uh, my contract is suspended? You know that according to the contract, you can only do that during financial difficulty for up to two months before the contract self-terminates with a small single-pay period compensation?" Dek looked down at papers on his desk then responded, "I know. For now, we will make use of that clause in the contract, and we will let you know if we need to terminate the contract. That is the best I can do for now. Leave any company project files in the usual places on the hard drive in case you return or we need to have another look at them. Please, clean up whatever you had going, and you can go for now."

That was a quick day at work; he had barely finished his coffee. Mark reached for the door and stepped outside. There was no noticeable difference at the office except that the parking lot showed fewer cars than usual for this time of day. The air was still, and noise was minimal. A few light, wispy clouds populated the otherwise blue sky as though the remnants of some high-speed travel path. There seemed to be a few birds chirping in the distance. Opening the car door, Mark positioned himself in the driver's seat, in one smooth motion. Mark felt a little more aware for some reason. There was a placid sense in the air, and it seemed as though Mark could sense every detail of his surroundings. He paused for an "in the moment" reflection then slipped his key-chip in the ignition. Mark swiftly made his way back home.

Pulling into the neat yet slightly dusty garage, Mark exited the car and waltzed through the door in a smoothly civil manner. He could not help but notice the empty location, like a void, where the three-dimensional art previously resided. The echo of its previous existence provided a reminder and made the room look incomplete. How annoying, he thought as he quickly located a statue of a purposely smooth, chiseled, and unfrilled falcon overlooking a smooth stone table surface to take its place. "There, that's better," Mark mumbled to himself. Turning to the den, he grabbed the mouse and turned his home entertainment system on then quickly reached for a scoop of gourmet coffee.

Sipping his coffee, Mark was observing the daily news when his tablet notified him of an incoming text. It was Ramses. "Guess what? The police have located my property!" Mark texted back, "Awesome, is Garrick with you?" Ramses replied, "Yes, me and Garrick are here. What's the scene there?" Mark texted back while taking another sip of his steaming coffee, "Well, my contract is suspended for now. Can I check your scene?" Ramses text replied, "See you soon!" Mark finished the coffee while grabbing his jacket and making for the door.

Mark swiftly drove a few blocks down the road; the nice thing was that Ramses lived nearby. Ramses' enormous driveway was nearly a parking lot, where the gray concrete had large edges of golden tan. The surrounding lawn had lush thickly bladed Bermuda grass, which intermixed with palm trees and sand. Stepping out of his Acura, Mark walked toward the front door; the multi-pathed walkway alone was as large as a four-lane highway. The walkway was a golden sand-colored concrete with a central bronze-colored marble pyramid. The pyramid had a constant stream of steaming hot water pouring from the top into the surrounding pool of water.

The house had large golden concrete blocks that appeared to be three stories high even though it actually was only two. The large glass door was tinted, having a faded bronze handle, purposely looking very old even though it was fairly new. Mark reached for the obvious touchpad on the door and touched it, causing a barely audible custom ringtone to sound from the inside.

Ramses opened the door. "Do, whazzup!" Garrick was standing just inside. "What's the flow?" Mark replied, smiling, as he entered the foyer. The foyer had a marble tiled floor with a naturally lit Plexiglas ceiling nearly thirty feet high. Garrick smiled widely. "Want some pizza? We're watching an action flick while we return Ramses' things to where they go." The three of them meandered into the enormous den that was colored with various creams, whites, and blacks. In the center, resting on the plush velvety cream carpeting, was a large quantity of boxes and furniture. Scanning the room, Mark commented, "Do, your dominion always seems so colossal even when it is small." Ramses smirked widely, a small tear forming, finally turning into a chuckle. "What can I say? It's my magic essence!" Then Mark turned to Ramses, laughing nearly to tears. "They really ran off with a lot of stuff. Really, they took all that?" Ramses smirked and reached for his head. "I know. I was a bit distraught. You should have seen it when the movers I hired first brought it in!"

The sun, moving ever so slowly, began to spray the den while luminous rays caused the entire room to look like some old museum or cream-colored tomb. Mark, pouring himself a Whiskey Seven, looked at Ramses. "So what's the story?" Ramses relaxed in a velvety chair and reached for his drink. "Apparently, there was some sort of thieving ring that has been rounded up. Fortunately for me, they arrested them before they had liquidated my things. Much more fortunate was my insurance company!" He smirked. They all laughed at that briefly. They spent the evening assisting Ramses with reorganizing his house.

Mark exited the house and walked towards his car. The moonlight danced on the steaming water fountain as if it was moving to some rhythm. The air was breezy and warm with a hint of tropical foliage reaching his nostrils. Mark revved the engine as he passed the gate assembly that Ramses had near the exit of the driveway with intent on increasing security to his house. The quick jaunt home was uneventful, and there was no one else on the road.

Reaching his house, Mark felt slightly different than usual, and he had felt that way all day. It was like he could sense every placid and active detail in the atmosphere; a sense of inner satisfaction made him feel extraordinarily enthusiastic for the coming day. Mark reached his comfortable large bed and relaxed. He was apparently tired because he very quickly shifted into the dream state.

Mark found himself drifting through a town. The town was similar to Olympus, yet different. The environment was a bit unusual, and Mark quickly determined he had less control of it. Mark drifted into a hospital, one he recognized as similar to the one in town, yet it was also different. The echoes of doctors and patients reverberated through the gleaming white hallway. Suddenly, Mark realized he could not control himself as much as in other dreams, and he involuntarily drifted into a hospital room.

Several people in basic attire were standing around, some of them praying while others announcing something about the gods. A doctor and a nurse in the usual white outfits stood near a bed, having a plastic curtain pulled all the way out of view. Finally, he could understand what they were saying. One man said, "He flatlined! Is he going to die? All this time, he has been in a coma. For some reason, I assumed he would eventually awaken." A woman said, "Jesus, help him!" The doctor holding a clipboard looked at the man and responded, “There was no real sign that he would die, and we have been doing everything we could to bring him out of the coma.” Mark moved into position, floating above where he could see the man in the bed.

Mark quickly recognized him; he was Chris Vocal, CEO of Applied Dynamics. Looking at the measurements, he noticed the flat line replacing the active ones, when suddenly they became active briefly, then repeated. The man exclaimed, “What can we do! What a letdown! All this time in a coma, and now suddenly, nearly without warning, flatline!” The doctor looked at him in a very serious manner. “I understand, we are doing all we can.” The nurse was administering some syringe to him.

Suddenly, the measurements came to life. The nurse jolted out of shock. Chris’s finger twitched a bit and his eyes began rolling under his eyelids. The man wearing some basic blue jeans, a T-shirt, and a baseball cap, who had spoken recently, asked with an emotional inflection in his tone, “Is he going to make it, or is it his last gasp?” Quickly, the nurse began to check his eyes.

Chris started spastic-ally jolting when his measurements normalized. The doctor exuberantly exclaimed, “I think he is going to make it!” Everyone in the room said, “Thank the gods!” Nearly without warning, Chris opened his eyes. “Wh-wh-where am I?” he said. Chris’s eyes rolled around like they were not reporting to the mind. Apparently, Chris was still blind. “Oh my god!” The man that had been talking previously nearly fell over. The doctor, clearly in shock, quickly stabilized. “Hi, Chris. You’re in the Braila Hospital. You had an accident a while ago, and you’ve been in a coma.”

The nurse jabbed, “Glad to have you back. You scared us for a minute there. We thought we were going to lose you.” Chris relaxed in his bed then said, “I had the weirdest dreams. I was in some place called Olympus where I owned a large company that was faltering . . . I-I had some powerful opponents. That much I remember.” One of the women spoke, “It’s over now. You’re here with us, back home in Braila.” Mark began to drift away from the hospital room when a loud noise interrupted him. Mark forcefully opened his eyes to the usual patterns in the ceiling.

Mark sat at the edge of the bed while turning off the alarm on his tablet. Light blasted in, causing natural warmth to permeate most of the room. Mark took a moment to look around the room. Everything was as he had left it, except for a few new spider webs.

Mark closed his eyes briefly and then opened them again. This time, his third eye opened with them. Suddenly, he could see all sorts of energies. Mark scrutinized what he was viewing, the imagery was sharp and clear nothing was warped at all. In fact, his senses were a bit more acute and he could see details he would not have normally been able to detect. While environmental energies exist everywhere, Mark had some unique ones in his domain.

Instantly, he noticed his room was full of spider webs and spiders in the thousands—spiders as large as a PlayStation. Mark reached to touch one that was sitting on his bed, staring at him. It was energy, all right. He could feel its texture. Immediately, it began acting like a munster sort of dog and rubbing itself against his hand. Mark stood up and made for the door. All the spiders looked at him and, in a limited sense, followed him around the room, yet they stayed in the room as he exited. Of course, he always knew they were there and was not really surprised.

Mark recalled the dream. "What a trip," he mumbled to himself while enjoying the velvety carpet. Meandering down the stairs, Mark reached the den where he clicked his television system on. Today was one of the first days for some time that Mark did not have a contract to work on. The news immediately started playing while Mark grabbed a scoop of espresso. The aroma of the espresso mixed with Mark's natural masculinity and the still-fresh carpet smell, which had been there since he had the carpets cleaned.

Groggily awakening from what seemed like a deep sleep all Tina could see was blackness. What happened, did I fall down? She thought to herself. She could hear some whispering voices nearby. Slowly she could make out some forms in the darkness; it appeared to be the basement. How did she get here? She slowly became aware that she was surrounded by dark cloud-like forms saying various things to each other.

One state to her, “You’ve crossed the threshold. Everything here only goes one way including light.” It reached out and touched her head. Suddenly, she could see nothing. “Until now I actually liked this place better than Olympus, I could start young again and everything.” Gasping she touched her eyes with her hand and could still not see anything. Was she blind? Just like that? All the black clouds started snickering and one said, “After were finished reprogramming you you’ll never know the difference. This will be fun for us; I can’t say the same for you.” A strange sensation overcame her head; it was cold and slightly painful like a headache. She suddenly lost consciousness.

Mark was sipping his espresso when his tablet notified him of a text. The television news shifted to breaking news. “Chris Vocal, CEO and owner of Applied Dynamics, was found deceased this morning. Chris apparently fell down the stairs, causing an internal head injury.” Mark smirked at the news while checking his tablet. “Call me when you have an opportunity.” It was Ben. Suddenly, an actual call was coming in, and Mark answered it.

“Mark? This is Dek from Applied Dynamics. Unfortunately, we will be terminating your contract. You will get your promised extra paycheck. Applied Dynamics is going into liquidation after the death of our owner and CEO. It was nice meeting you.” Dek had a very matter-of-fact tone, and there was no video. Mark replied, “Okay, I kind of had a feeling that things weren’t as great as they could be there. Thank you for letting me know.” “Have a good day,” Dek finalized the conversation then hung up.

Mark sipped his espresso with a moment of warmth then called Ben. “Hello, Ben. How are you on this fine day?” Mark zapped with a smile. Ben smirked jovially. “Well, Applied Dynamics apparently has termed your contract.” Mark chuckled. “Yes, I got off the phone with them only moments ago. Not every company liquidates after the owner chokes, or in this case, takes a trip.” Ben, serious yet still smiling, said, “Yeah, that is true. That company is quickly dissolving, however. You have plenty of funds on hand, though, don’t you? I doubt you’re shakin’ in your boots!” Mark wiped his forehead in jest, still smirking. “I’m fine, and I have more money than before, actually. My account sizzles right now.” Ben chuckled. “Okay, well, how about you take a break and enjoy it. When you’re ready, call me. I’ll have some choice contract options.” Mark smirked. “Will do, will do, friend.”

Jolting, Mark dropped his tablet on the counter by the interruption of an intruder. "Hello, good morning, beautiful!" Mairis announced. Mark braced himself on the counter. "Oh, you surprised me. Good morning! A good morning for you to come over since I have plenty in my bank account, and my contract has been termed." Mairis smiled confidently. "You'll have a new contract, I assume?" Mark made a slow beaming smirk. "That's the great news. Apparently, I'll have some really nice options. I, just moments ago, discussed it with Ben. However, not until after I take a nice break to enjoy my new house and money." Mairis touched her mouth while stepping back with a slightly seductive look. "Seems like that is what we need to do then. I am ready to do whatever!"

Afterword

Many of the scenarios in this book come from actual dream and non-dream experiences. This story has been formatted to be an interesting story, and I hope you liked it. Preferably, it has inspired you with the possibilities of what may be, where we can be, and where we have been. While we all create our own little universe, there are those universes designed by others that we will want to interact with, and those that we do not. Plan wisely, but don't leave out the thrill of connecting.

Printed in the United States
by Baker & Taylor Publisher Services